UNFRIENDLY FIRE

"Don't shoot!" Fargo yelled, but sparks geysered from the barrel of the rifle as the man pulled the trigger anyway. Fargo was already using his knees to swerve the stallion to the side. The move came just in time. He heard the flat *whap!* of the bullet passing by his head, much too close for comfort.

"Hold your fire, damn it!" Fargo shouted again, but he could see that the bearded man was already levering another shell into the rifle's chamber. Fargo didn't want to have to shoot the man, but he wasn't going to just let himself be ventilated, either. With a yell, he sent the Ovaro lunging forward in a gallop, straight at the man with the rifle.

The man triggered another shot, but it went wild. Fargo knew that hitting something coming straight at you was one of the most difficult shots to make. He veered the horse to the side again, kicked his feet free of the stirrups, and left the saddle in a diving tackle that sent him crashing into the rifleman. . . .

THE
TRAILSMAN
#256

HIGH COUNTRY
HORROR

by

Jon Sharpe

A SIGNET BOOK

SIGNET
Published by New American Library, a division of
Penguin Putnam Inc., 375 Hudson Street,
New York, New York 10014, U.S.A.
Penguin Books Ltd, 80 Strand,
London WC2R 0RL, England
Penguin Books Australia Ltd, 250 Camberwell Road,
Camberwell, Victoria 3124, Australia
Penguin Books Canada Ltd, 10 Alcorn Avenue,
Toronto, Ontario, Canada M4V 3B2
Penguin Books (N.Z.) Ltd, Cnr Rosedale and Airborne Roads,
Albany, Auckland 1310, New Zealand

Penguin Books Ltd, Registered Offices:
Harmondsworth, Middlesex, England

First published by Signet, an imprint of New American Library,
a division of Penguin Putnam Inc.

First Printing, February 2003
10   9   8   7   6   5   4   3   2   1

The first chapter of this title originally appeared in *Montana Madmen*,
the two hundred fifty-fifth volume in this series.

REGISTERED TRADEMARK—MARCA REGISTRADA

Printed in the United States of America

PUBLISHER'S NOTE
This is a work of fiction. Names, characters, places, and incidents either
are the product of the author's imagination or are used fictitiously,
and any resemblance to actual persons, living or dead, events, or locales
is entirely coincidental.

The Trailsman

Beginnings . . . they bend the tree and they mark the man. Skye Fargo was born when he was eighteen. Terror was his midwife, vengeance his first cry. Killing spawned Skye Fargo, ruthless, cold-blooded murder. Out of the acrid smoke of gunpowder still hanging in the air, he rose, cried out a promise never forgotten.

The Trailsman they began to call him all across the West: searcher, scout, hunter, the man who could see where others only looked, his skills for hire but not his soul, the man who lived each day to the fullest, yet trailed each tomorrow. Skye Fargo, the Trailsman, the seeker who could take the wildness of a land and the wanting of a woman and make them his own.

The high country, Washington Territory, 1860—
Where the hopes and dreams of
pilgrims on the Oregon Trail
fall prey to the greed of evil men.

1

It had been too long, Skye Fargo thought as he reined the big black-and-white stallion to a halt. Too long since he had seen these rugged mountains that loomed before him, their rocky, snow-capped summits reaching toward the brilliantly blue sky above them. Fargo drew in a deep breath of the clean, crisp, cold air, savoring it. He thought he smelled snow, but that could have been his imagination since the sky was clear. He patted the Ovaro's shoulder. The magnificent horse nickered in a companionable fashion, as if to say that he enjoyed the spectacular view as much as Fargo did.

But then the lake-blue eyes of the big man in buckskins narrowed as a frown creased his forehead. Something was wrong.

Some people said that Skye Fargo had the keenest eyesight and the sharpest hearing of any man west of the Mississippi—and probably east of the Father of Waters, too. That was why he was the best tracker and trailsman to be found. Fargo had never really believed that of himself; no matter how good a man was at anything, there was always somebody out there somewhere in the world who was better. He knew he had good eyes and ears, though. He had to, in order to have lived as long as he had on the frontier. Now those senses told him there was something amiss about the scene before him, and as he leaned forward in the saddle, he realized what it was.

He was in southeastern Washington Territory, on the

edge of the Snake River Plain northwest of Fort Hall, one of the stops along the Oregon Trail, the great immigrant trace that led from Independence, Missouri, to the Pacific Northwest. But Fargo was facing north at the moment, looking toward the Sawtooth Mountains and the Lost River Range. The Oregon Trail was behind him. There shouldn't have been any wagon trains in this part of the country, especially not at this time of year. It was late fall, and winter could come crashing down at any time with little or no warning.

Unless he was seeing things, though, those tiny white dots moving into the mountains in the distance were wagons. The bleached canvas covers over the wagon beds stood out sharply against the greens, browns, grays, and blues of the wilderness landscape.

"What in blazes are a bunch of pilgrims doing up here?" Fargo asked the Ovaro. He didn't think there was anything unusual about talking aloud to the horse. The two of them were longtime companions, and the stallion had been a better friend to Fargo than many of the humans he had known. Unfortunately, the horse couldn't answer him in words. The Ovaro tossed his head, however, as if he shared Fargo's concern.

"Yeah," Fargo said. "Reckon we'd better go take a look."

The wagon train was miles away, and even though Fargo knew that he and the stallion could make much better time than those slow-moving prairie schooners, he realized it might be dark before he caught up to them. The emigrants would stop and camp when night fell, but Fargo could continue on. He had no doubt he would be able to locate the wagons. The travelers would build cooking fires, and the sight of the flames and the smell of the smoke would serve as beacons.

Those pilgrims had better hope that he was the only one drawn to their camp, Fargo thought. The Shoshones had been pretty peaceful of late, but there was no way of knowing when some of the young warriors might take it into their heads to run off some horses for fun. A raid on the wagon train, even a raid that the Indians didn't take completely seriously, could lead to shooting, and that could cause some real problems.

Fargo told himself not to borrow trouble. He put the Ovaro into a ground-eating lope and started making up the distance between the wagons and him.

As he expected, darkness settled over the landscape before he caught up to the wagon train. That slowed him down, because the moon had not yet risen. Fargo could navigate by starlight, but not as well as by day. Tonight, the moon would be almost full. Once it was up, he would be able to increase his pace again.

As he rode, he thought about possible explanations for the odd sight he was on his way to investigate. He supposed that a wagon train could have strayed off the main trail and headed north into the mountains, thinking they were going the right way. That was unlikely, though. Most groups of emigrants hired experienced guides to lead them to what they hoped would be their promised land. Fargo himself had guided more than one wagon train across the frontier. No guide worth his salt could have gotten so turned around, and not many would still be traveling with winter about to come on, unless they knew they were close enough to their destination to risk it.

Maybe there was a new trail he didn't know about. It had been a while since he'd been in this part of the country. It might be the pilgrims in the wagon train were on their way to a new settlement somewhere up yonder in the valley of the Big Lost River. Fargo didn't think that was the case, though. At the head of that valley were some of the tallest, most rugged peaks in these parts. The valley wasn't really good farming or ranching land. This was fur-trapping country, or at least it had been before hordes of mountain men had journeyed to the region back in the thirties and forties and taken most of the beaver plews. Fargo seemed to recall hearing about a trappers' fort being located somewhere in this area, but it had long since been abandoned. Some trapping still went on, but the fur industry wasn't the power it had once been.

3

No, the more he turned it over in his head, the less reason Fargo could see for those wagons to be heading into the mountains. A feeling of unease began to grow inside him as he climbed to a narrow pass and rode through it into the Big Lost River valley. Out here on the frontier, something that didn't have a good explanation usually had a bad one. He urged the Ovaro into a little faster gait, even though the light still wasn't good.

He had ridden less than a mile when he heard an ominous popping in the distance. The sounds were faint but recognizable.

Gunshots.

"Damn it," Fargo grated. He heeled the stallion into a trot. Even though it was dark, he had to make tracks now. There was trouble up ahead.

But he couldn't help anybody if the horse stumbled and fell and broke a leg or went lame. He would then be afoot and wouldn't be able to reach the wagons for hours. He had to hold the Ovaro back from the breakneck pace the stallion would have adopted if Fargo had given him his head. Fargo had to balance the need to reach his destination safely against the urge to hurry.

The shooting died away after a short time. Fargo bit back another curse. Whatever had happened up there at the emigrant camp, it was over now. Maybe he wouldn't be too late to help. All he could do was hope.

More than an hour after the sun went down, Fargo spotted a good-sized fire up ahead. By now the moon was up, casting silvery illumination over the twisting trail on which Fargo rode. He was already moving fast, but when he saw the fire he let the Ovaro run. The path he had to follow through the winding valley cut him off from sight of the blaze from time to time, but he was always able to find it again. Something big was burning.

He had penetrated miles into the valley before he reached the spot. The Sawtooths rose toweringly to his left, the Lost River Range flanked him on the right. The valley was pretty narrow in most places, with just enough level ground alongside the river for the wagons to travel, but it widened out here and there, and the wagons had

4

come to a stop in one of the wider areas. They had been pulled into a circle with the livestock in the middle, as usual. Fargo estimated the number of wagons at a dozen. One of them was still on fire, and the garish glare from the flames revealed that two more of the vehicles were nothing but burned-out husks. Quite a few people were standing around watching the blaze, not even trying to put out the flames. Fargo guessed they figured the burning wagon was too far gone to save, even though the river was nearby.

Some of the bystanders must have heard the pounding of the Ovaro's hooves over the crackling and popping of the conflagration, because several of them turned toward Fargo. One of them, a man with a bushy black beard, was holding a rifle. To Fargo's surprise, the man jerked the weapon to his shoulder and started drawing a bead on him.

"Don't shoot!" Fargo yelled, but sparks geysered from the barrel of the rifle as the man pulled the trigger. Fargo was already using his knees to swerve the stallion to the side. The move came just in time. He heard the flat *whap!* of the bullet passing by his head, much too close for comfort.

"Hold your fire, damn it!" Fargo shouted again, but he could see that the bearded man was already levering another shell into the rifle's chamber. The weapon was a Henry repeater like the one Fargo carried, and fully loaded it held fifteen rounds. Fargo didn't want to have to shoot the man, but he wasn't going to just let himself be ventilated, either. With a yell, he sent the Ovaro lunging forward in a gallop, straight at the man with the rifle.

The man triggered another shot, but it went wild. Fargo knew that hitting something coming straight at you was one of the most difficult shots to make. The stallion covered the rest of the ground between Fargo and the rifleman as the man was trying to work the weapon's lever. Fargo veered the horse to the side again, kicked his feet free of the stirrups, and left the saddle in a diving tackle that sent him crashing into the rifleman. The impact of the collision sent the man flying backward off his feet. Fargo landed on top of him, knocking the breath out of the man's lungs. He lay there on the ground, stunned and gasping for air, unable to put up a fight as Fargo jerked the Henry out of his hands and rolled off to the side. Fargo was a little shaken, too, but he didn't allow that to slow him down as he came to his feet and whirled to face the rest of the pilgrims. The rifle was in his hands, ready for use if he needed it. He didn't want to shoot any of these people unless he had to, and even then, he would try to wound, rather than kill.

It took only a second for Fargo to realize that the rest of the crowd represented no threat to him. They were all standing around gaping. Quite a few of them were women and children. Several of the men seemed to be wounded. Fargo saw bloodstains on their clothes and crude bandages wrapped around arms and legs and heads. None of them appeared to be armed. The Henry rifle he was now holding seemed to be the only gun left in the camp.

Fargo raised his voice so that they could hear him over the noise of the burning wagon. "You folks take it easy! I'm here to help you if I can, not to cause more trouble for you."

One of the women took a tentative step forward. "You're not another thief?"

"No, ma'am," Fargo assured her. "I heard the shooting and figured there was trouble up here, so I caught up to you as fast as I could."

"You're a . . . liar!" The choked-out words came from behind Fargo, from the bearded man he had knocked down. "You're . . . one of them!"

Fargo stepped to the side and turned so that he could look down at the man. "One of who?" he asked.

"Those bastards . . . working with Corrigan! Damned thieves!"

"I don't know who Corrigan is," Fargo said. "And I'm not a thief. My name is Fargo. Skye Fargo."

"The one called the Trailsman?" The startled question

came from the woman who had spoken a moment earlier.

Fargo turned back toward her and nodded. "Some have called me that," he admitted.

"Where we started back in Missouri, everyone said we should hire you as our guide if we could find you," the woman said. She shook her head. "But you weren't available, and it was getting late in the season already. We figured we'd better take whoever we could get and get started if we were going to."

"And look what it got us," the man on the ground said bitterly. He pushed himself into a sitting position. "Two of our number killed! Our wagons looted and burned! And the lot of us abandoned to die in the wilderness!"

"You're not going to die in the wilderness," Fargo said. "You're in a bad fix, but it's not hopeless." He lowered the Henry, sensing that the situation had calmed down somewhat. "I'll give you a hand getting wherever you're going."

The woman moved closer to him. "We're bound for Oregon, of course."

Fargo shook his head. "Not by going this way, you're not. You're heading straight into some of the most rugged country in the Rockies."

"Damn that Corrigan!" the bearded man said. "Not only is he a thief, but he didn't even know where he was going!"

"I doubt that," Fargo said with a shrug. "From what I gather, the hombre must have planned this out pretty carefullike. Why don't some of you tell me exactly what happened, while the rest of you make sure that fire doesn't spread to any of the other wagons? Fill some buckets at the river and wet down the rest of the wagons as much as you can."

The bearded man got to his feet. "You heard the man," he said grudgingly to the others. "Let's try to save what we can."

The woman came up to Fargo. "I can tell you what happened, Mr. Fargo."

The bearded man pushed between them. "Blast it, Maureen, let me handle this. This ain't woman's business."

For a second, Fargo thought the woman called Maureen was going to take a swing at the bearded man. He wouldn't have minded seeing that. But with a visible effort, she controlled her anger. "You should mind what you say, Milo," she told him. "That mouth of yours has gotten you in trouble before."

The man glared at her. "By thunder, if you weren't my brother's wife—"

"I'm your brother's widow," she said softly. "Daniel is dead, remember?"

The man reached up and scrubbed a hand across his face. He sighed. "Of course I remember," he said. "I'm sorry." He looked at Fargo. "And I reckon I'm sorry I took a shot at you, too, mister. I thought you were one of those robbers coming back to plague us again."

"Forget it," Fargo said, even though the apology had been delivered with ill grace and not a lot of sincerity. He picked up his hat, which had fallen off when he tackled Milo, and settled it on his thick black hair. "Why don't both of you fill me in on what happened?"

"Come over to my wagon," Maureen said.

Fargo took hold of the Ovaro's reins and fell in step beside her. He studied her in the light from the burning wagon as he walked across the camp with her and Milo, who was evidently her brother-in-law. Former brother-in-law, rather, since Maureen had said that her husband, Milo's brother, was dead. She was of medium height, between twenty-five and thirty years old, and had thick brown hair that fell to her shoulders and framed an attractive face. Her jaw was a bit too wide for her to be a classic beauty, but Fargo thought she was mighty nice-looking anyway. It had been his experience that women whose looks were perfect seldom matched that standard in other ways. Maureen's eyes held intelligence and the strength to deal with adversity, and to Fargo, that made her more attractive than many of the women he'd met.

"There's coffee, if it hasn't all boiled away," she said

as the three of them came up to one of the wagons. "I had just put it on to heat when the trouble started."

"Coffee sounds just fine," Fargo said in response to the implied offer. He looped the stallion's reins around a wheel spoke. He would need to unsaddle the horse and rub him down later, but for now the Ovaro was all right.

Maureen got tin cups from the wagon. She used a thick piece of leather to protect her hand as she picked up a coffeepot from the glowing embers at the edge of a small fire. She filled a cup, handed it to Fargo, then did likewise for Milo. Fargo said, "Thanks," but Milo just grunted.

The coffee had been boiling for a while and was pretty potent, but Fargo didn't mind. He sipped the steaming black brew and then said, "I reckon this fella Corrigan you mentioned was your guide?"

Milo nodded. "That's right. He pretended to be, anyway. Actually, he was nothing but a low-down, no-good thief."

"He seemed fine until tonight," Maureen added. "Then he announced that he was leaving us here and taking all our money and valuables. I thought he was just joking at first, although it certainly wasn't very humorous."

"And then some other men came out of the darkness and pointed guns at us," Milo said. "We knew then that Corrigan was serious."

The story held no surprises for Fargo so far. "Corrigan led you right into a trap. He had a gang of owl hoots waiting here for you."

"That's right." Maureen's voice shook. "There were at least half a dozen of them. And then Tom Dodd . . ." Her voice trailed away, and she couldn't go on.

"Tom Dodd pulled a gun on them." Milo took up the story. "Tom was a good man, as solid a fellow as you'd ever want to meet, but he was no gunfighter. A couple of those outlaws blew him right out of his boots. Mitchell Weems grabbed his shotgun and tried to open up on them, but they gunned him down before he could get a shot off.

There was a lot of shooting, and some of our men were wounded by stray bullets. After that . . ." Milo shook his head. "After that, we all just figured it would be better to cooperate, before somebody else got killed."

Fargo's face was solemn as he nodded. "You did the right thing. Desperadoes like that wouldn't think anything of killing all of you if you'd kept putting up a fight. You're really pretty lucky. Some gangs would have wiped you out just so they wouldn't be leaving any witnesses behind."

"Tom and Mitchell's wives and children don't feel very lucky, I imagine," Maureen said.

"No, of course not. I didn't mean to downplay your losses. I'm just saying it could have been even worse."

"Those bastards took everything we had," Milo said. "All our cash, our jewelry, our guns, all the supplies they could carry . . . They left us in a mighty bad fix, Mr. Fargo." Now that his anger had subsided, he was starting to sound worried. "How will we get out of these mountains and back to civilization?"

"They left your livestock," Fargo pointed out. "Fort Hall is less than a week from here, even traveling slow. There's plenty of game between here and there. Nobody will starve on the way. You'll likely have to winter there, though. No place else close enough where you could ride out what's coming."

Maureen put a hand on his buckskin-clad arm. "You'll guide us, Mr. Fargo?"

He nodded. "Sure. I was at loose ends right now anyway, looking for a place to winter myself."

"We can't pay you anything," Milo said gruffly.

"Don't worry about it," Fargo said with a faint smile. He lifted his cup. "I reckon some good coffee and good company is payment enough for my time and trouble."

Maureen laughed. "The coffee's better when I'm not being held up by outlaws in the middle of heating it. As for the company, well, we'll do what we can."

The light was uncertain, but Fargo thought he saw a hint of a bold gleam in her eyes as she spoke.

She held out her hand. "You told us your name, but

we haven't actually been introduced. I'm Maureen Haydon, and this is my brother-in-law Milo Haydon."

Fargo shook hands with both of them. "Pleased to meet you. I wish it had been under better circumstances."

"That's the damned truth," Milo said. "I'm the one who put this bunch together, and I'll bet right now they're thinking I sure have let them down."

"It wasn't your fault Mr. Corrigan turned out to be a treacherous thief," Maureen told him.

"I should've figured out that we've been going the wrong way since we left Fort Hall, though. My God, can't I tell one direction from another?"

Fargo thought somebody in the wagon train should have noticed, too, but it wasn't going to help matters for them to sit around and cast blame. Deal with things the way they were, not the way you wish they were—that was one of his rules.

"Tell me about Corrigan," he said. "Did he sign on all the way back in Missouri?"

Maureen shook her head. "No, we picked him up at Fort Laramie. A man named Jenkins had guided us that far from Independence, Missouri, but he broke his leg in an accident there and couldn't carry on. That left us to find whoever we could who claimed to know the trail. Mr. Corrigan fit the bill."

Fargo cast his thoughts back through his memory. "I know most of the men who guide wagon trains along the Oregon Trail. Don't remember any Corrigan."

"Tall fellow with long sandy hair," Milo said, supplying the description. "Wears buckskins sort of like yours, but he has a brown hat with a really tall crown and silver buttons around the band."

Fargo shook his head. "Nope, doesn't sound familiar. Reckon I never ran into him before."

"I'd like to see him again," Milo said. "Over the sights of my rifle."

Fargo still had the Henry tucked under his left arm. He handed it back to Milo. "You said the gang took all your guns. Where did this rifle come from?"

"It was in the back of my wagon, underneath a pile of other things. When they were searching, they just didn't find it, thank God."

Fargo didn't point out the obvious, that the Henry hadn't done Milo any good stashed in the back of a wagon with a lot of things piled on top of it. Anyway, he thought, if the rifle had been handy, Milo probably would be dead now, too, because Fargo didn't think the man could have resisted the temptation to try making a play against the robbers.

A few small campfires were still burning, but the wagon that had been on fire when Fargo rode up was no longer blazing. It was nothing more than a charred frame and wheels now. The emigrants were standing around looking at the destruction, stunned expressions on their faces. Somebody needed to take this bunch in hand, and Fargo suspected it wasn't going to be Milo. Maureen would make a better leader, he judged, but most of the men wouldn't take orders from a woman.

"Everybody needs to see what supplies they have left," Fargo suggested, raising his voice so that the whole group could hear him. "That way you'll know what kind of shape you're in for the trip back to Fort Hall. Tend to the livestock if you haven't done that already. And you'd better post a couple of guards just in case of more trouble."

"What'll we use for weapons?" one of the men asked. "Those bandits took everything."

"Milo here still has a Henry rifle, and so do I," Fargo said. "Whoever's standing sentry duty will be armed with them. Better take mighty good care of them, since they're the only long guns we've got left." Fargo turned to Milo and lowered his voice. "What about the two men who were killed?"

"What about 'em?"

"I figure you'll want to see that they have a proper burial."

"Of course," Maureen said. "We're all just so . . . so upset, it's hard to think straight."

"You'll have to get over that," Fargo said, knowing

he was speaking bluntly. "You should be able to get back to the fort, and I'll do what I can to help you, but from here on out everybody will have to be as alert and clearheaded as possible."

"You're right," Milo said. "I'll get some of the men started digging a couple of graves."

Fargo had to prod some of the emigrants again, but over the next half hour he got everyone in the wagon train busy. The children took care of the stock, the women resumed the interrupted task of preparing supper, and the men split up to inventory what was left in the wagons, dig graves for the two dead pilgrims, and post some guards. The atmosphere that hung over the camp was a somber one, but Fargo knew it was better for them to be doing things rather than just sitting around feeling sorry for themselves.

The wind picked up and seemed to grow colder. Fargo looked up at the moon and saw clouds streaking across its glowing face. As he watched, the racing clouds almost completely obscured it. The air had a raw feeling.

Fargo's jaw tightened, but he didn't say anything. No sense in worrying the others just yet. Besides, he could still be wrong about what was coming.

But less than ten minutes later, he felt something cold touch his face. He looked up, saw the snowflakes beginning to swirl down from the heavens, and knew that things had just gone from bad to worse. Much worse.

2

The storm wasn't as bad here in the mountains as it would have been out on the prairie. The peaks provided some shelter from the howling, biting wind that swept down out of the north. But it was bad enough, Fargo knew. The wagons couldn't travel in it, and there was a good chance that by morning the narrow pass leading into the southern end of the valley would be blocked by high, thick drifts of snow.

Fargo's nose hadn't been wrong when he'd thought he smelled snow that afternoon, but he took no comfort from the vindication. This was one time when he would rather have been mistaken. The harsh winter weather was going to make his self-appointed job of getting the wagon train back to Fort Hall a lot more difficult.

It was hard to keep cooking fires burning in the snow and the wind, and after a while everyone gave up and retreated into the wagons to make a cold supper of jerky and stale biscuits. Milo Haydon came up to Fargo while he was spreading a blanket over the unsaddled back of the Ovaro and lifted his voice to be heard over the wind.

"Maureen sent me to tell you to come to her wagon to get out of the storm!"

Fargo nodded and cinched the blanket in place. The stallion was a hardy animal. He felt confident the big horse could ride out the storm without much trouble if it didn't last too long. Often, these first storms of the winter blew over quickly. Maybe it wouldn't be too bad,

Fargo told himself. He didn't have a very good feeling about it, though.

The idea of spending the night in Maureen's wagon was appealing, but it also seemed a mite improper. Not to Fargo, necessarily, but it might appear that way to the other people in the wagon train. He wasn't going to have to worry about being unchaperoned, he saw, as he made his way to the rear of the wagon. Milo came with him and clearly had every intention of joining Fargo and Maureen inside.

They climbed over the tailgate and pushed aside the canvas flaps that had been drawn closed to keep out as much of the snow and wind as possible. A lantern was burning inside. It gave off a little heat, but not much. Maureen was sitting on a bunk built into one side of the wagon bed. She had a heavy quilt drawn around her shoulders.

"Welcome, Mr. Fargo," she said. "I'm sorry we can't offer you any better accommodations."

Fargo grinned. "On a night like this, ma'am, the back of a wagon is downright cozy." He was carrying his saddlebags. He hunkered on his heels and took out a paper-wrapped package. "I've got some salt jowl here that was cooked yesterday. Be glad to share it."

"That sounds wonderful. Thank you."

Fargo slid his Arkansas toothpick from the sheath in his boot and used the keen blade to carve strips off the jowl. He handed the first ones to Maureen, then gave some to Milo, who grunted, "Thanks."

Fargo chewed a while on the tough but tasty meat and washed it down with more coffee from the pot that Maureen had brought inside the wagon. The coffee was cold now, but Fargo didn't care. He ate a biscuit that Maureen gave him and listened to the wind blowing outside.

"It sounds almost like wolves howling," she said.

Fargo nodded. "Yep, but if you were to hear a real wolf right now, you'd be able to tell the difference. Sometimes it does seem like the wind's almost alive, though."

15

"What's going to happen to us?" Milo asked. "If the snow piles up deep, will the wagons be able to get through?"

"Maybe, but the pass out of here is what worries me," Fargo said. "The snow will drift there, and it may be too high to get past. In that case, we won't be able to get out of the valley to the south."

"What'll we do? Wait for the snow to melt?"

Fargo considered that for a moment. "We could give that a try. At this time of year, it's possible the weather might warm up again, at least enough to melt some of the snowdrift. But it might take a while." He shrugged. "Might not melt at all. I've known the passes in the high country to be blocked from this time of year until the spring thaw."

"But . . . but we'll *starve*. We don't have enough supplies to feed everybody for months! We barely have enough left for a few days."

"Mr. Fargo said there was plenty of game around here," Maureen pointed out.

"Plenty if you were just making a run back to Fort Hall," Fargo said. He rubbed his bearded jaw and frowned in thought. "I don't know about lasting out the winter."

"Oh, my God." Maureen's voice was hushed. "You mean we really might starve to death up here?"

"We're a long way from having to worry about that," Fargo said quickly.

Milo gave an angry snort. "You're a fine one to talk, Fargo. You can get on your horse and ride out of here any time you want. You don't have to worry about getting a bunch of wagons out."

Fargo felt a prickle of irritation at Milo's attitude. "That's right," he snapped. "I can ride out any time I want, once this storm blows over. But I'm not going to. I said I'd help you folks, and I meant it."

Milo looked like he was about to say something else, but Maureen put a hand on his shoulder to stop him. "We appreciate your help, Mr. Fargo," she said. She gave Milo a meaningful glance. "I know I speak for everyone when I say that."

"I haven't actually done anything yet," Fargo said.

"But we all have confidence in you. If anyone can get us to safety, it's the famous Trailsman."

Fargo looked down into his coffee cup. There were times when having a reputation came in handy, and there were other times it was a damned nuisance. He would do what he could for these pilgrims, but he was only human. They didn't need to be looking at him like he was some sort of savior.

"We'll see how bad things are in the morning," he said. "In the meantime, why don't you tell me where you're from?"

"Illinois," Maureen said. "Milo put the group together last spring. It took us longer than we thought it would to get to Independence, though, and then the trip across the plains was difficult, too."

"My brother Dan always wanted to come west," Milo said, and now his tone was less gruff, more relaxed and almost sentimental. "We figured on coming out here together, but that didn't work out. Still, Maureen and me, we figured we ought to carry on . . ."

"I didn't mean to open up any old wounds," Fargo said as he caught a glimpse of tears shining in Maureen's eyes.

"No, that's all right," she told him. "It's been over a year now. I suppose the pain of losing Daniel will always be there for both of us, but we're getting along all right. Aren't we, Milo?"

Milo just grunted again. That seemed to be a common response for him, no matter what the question was.

"Daniel drowned in the Little Wabash, near our farm," Maureen went on. "It was flooding from the spring rains, and he was trying to move some of our cows to higher ground. It was terrible."

"I tried to save him," Milo said. "But he washed away before I could get a good grip on him. Lord knows how many times I've woke up since then, dreaming that if I had just held on tighter . . ."

Maureen squeezed his arm as his words died away. "Neither of us wanted to stay in Illinois after that. Milo

17

and Daniel were the only ones left in their family, so there was nothing to hold Milo there. I have relatives in Peoria, but I'm not close to them anymore. The idea of coming west was just so appealing. So we pooled our money and recruited other people to travel with us, and, well, here we are."

Fargo nodded. "Too bad the West hasn't given you a better welcome."

After a moment of silence, Maureen said, "What about you, Mr. Fargo? You strike me as a man who was born and raised out here on the frontier. Where are you from?"

Fargo smiled faintly. Despite all his wanderings, the past was one place he didn't go. "I don't rightly remember," he said. "You could just say I'm from all over."

"I see." Maureen still looked a little curious, but she didn't press the issue. Instead she changed the subject. "It's getting awfully cold."

"You need yourself a buffalo robe, like the Indians use," Fargo told her. "That'll keep you warm no matter how cold the temperature gets, as long as you don't mind the smell. And maybe a few bugs."

Maureen laughed. "Right now I wouldn't mind at all. I suppose we'll have to make do with quilts and blankets, though." She yawned and went on, "I'm about ready to turn in."

"Fargo and me will sleep on the floor," Milo said quickly.

Maureen stood up and opened a cedar chest on the other side of the wagon. "Let me get some covers for you."

Fargo had his own bedroll, but he had stashed it underneath the wagon. He used the quilts and blankets Maureen took from the cedar chest to make a comfortable pallet on the floor of the wagon. Milo did likewise. When they were set, Maureen slipped, fully dressed, under the covers on the bunk and leaned over to blow out the lantern. "Good night, Milo," she said. "Good night, Mr. Fargo."

"Call me Skye."

"All right. Good night, Skye." With a puff of breath, Maureen blew out the flame, and utter darkness descended on the wagon's interior.

Fargo didn't go to sleep immediately. He lay there and listened to Milo's breathing deepen and knew that slumber had claimed the man. Maureen's breathing was lighter as the sound of it came from the bunk, but it became deeper and more regular, too, as she dozed off. Finally, Fargo closed his eyes and slept, and the last thing he was aware of was the cry of the snow-laden wind outside the wagon.

When he awoke the next morning, the silence told him right away that the storm was over. That came as no surprise.

The surprise was that his arms were full of a warm female form.

The sudden stiffening of his muscles must have told Maureen he was awake. Lying with her back to him and his arms around her, she stirred sleepily and lifted her head a little. The scent of her hair filled Fargo's senses. "Good morning," she murmured.

Fargo raised his head to look around the inside of the wagon. Enough light came through the gap between the canvas flaps at the ends of the vehicle for him to see that Milo was gone. He wondered if Maureen had slipped into his covers while her brother-in-law was still there. He hoped she had been discreet enough to wait until she and Fargo were alone. He wondered as well why he hadn't woken up when she crawled in with him. He must have been really exhausted, he decided. Also, his instincts would have warned him if he had been in any danger, so deep down he must have known that Maureen was no threat. Most of the time—not always, but most of the time—when a woman climbed into Fargo's bed the only mischief she had in mind was the sensuous kind. Fargo wasn't convinced that was what Maureen Haydon was after, but he had to admit that it felt mighty good to be holding her like this. Her slender body was molded all up and down against his.

"Good morning," Fargo said. "I didn't expect to find you here, Mrs. Haydon."

"If I have to call you Skye, you have to call me Maureen." She shifted again, nestling her backside closer against his groin. "Do you want me to get up, Skye?"

Fargo chuckled. "You don't hear me complaining, do you?"

His manhood was beginning to stiffen, and she had to feel the shaft's hard prod against the softness of her rump. She didn't move away or start to carry on. Instead she made a low noise of contentment deep in her throat. "It's been so long since a man held me like this," she whispered. "So long . . ."

Fargo's arms tightened around her. He bent his head slightly so that he could kiss the back of her neck. His lips trailed around the side of her head and nuzzled the lobe of her ear. She sighed.

"I wish . . . I wish there was time . . . and a place where we could be alone for a while . . ."

"Maybe there will be," Fargo told her. "When this is all over . . ."

Voices sounded outside, not close to the wagon but loud enough to make Maureen's body go tense in Fargo's embrace. "I'd better get up," she said.

Fargo moved his arms so that he was no longer holding her. "All right."

Maureen turned so that she was facing him. She pressed her lips to his in a quick, urgent kiss. "You probably think I'm the world's biggest hussy," she said, "but I can't help it."

"What I think is that you're a smart, beautiful woman who's been lonely for too long," Fargo told her.

She smiled, kissed him again, and then pushed the covers aside so that she could get to her feet. Fargo sat up as Maureen went to the back of the wagon, pushed the flaps aside, and climbed out. He got his hat and followed her.

A few people were moving around the circled wagons. A couple of fires were burning, and Milo was carrying an armload of wood to one of them. He saw Fargo and

Maureen emerge from the wagon and gave them a curt nod. "Thought you two were going to sleep half the day away," he said as he dumped the broken branches onto the ground next to the fire.

Fargo glanced up at the sky. It was still overcast, but the clouds didn't seem to be as thick as they had been the night before when the storm hit. They might break up and show some sun before the day was over. Fargo judged it wasn't more than an hour past dawn. His breath fogged in front of his face. The temperature was below freezing. The snow wasn't melting at all and probably wouldn't today, he thought. He fetched his sheepskin jacket from his bedroll under the wagon and slipped into it, grateful for the added protection it provided against the cold.

The big black-and-white stallion nickered a friendly greeting when Fargo checked on him. The Ovaro had made it through the night without any trouble, as Fargo had expected. A quick look at the rest of the livestock penned in the center of the circle told him that the same was true of the other horses, the oxen, and the mules. These emigrants could have had it a lot worse, Fargo thought. At least they still had a chance for survival, though that chance had been better before the snow came.

Over the next hour, everyone got up, and more fires were built. At Fargo's suggestion, the travelers brought out all the supplies the outlaws had left them, and the provisions were pooled and placed in one of the wagons. "It'll be easier this way to keep up with what we have left and ration it out as needed. Everybody will share and share alike, and nobody does without."

"That ain't fair to those of us who got more," one of the men said.

Fargo gave him a hard look. "It's not fair to let somebody starve to death because Corrigan's gang stole more from him than they did from you, either," he said. "This is just until we get all of you back to Fort Hall or some other outpost."

Milo spoke up. "I've been wondering about that, Fargo. Isn't there any place closer?"

Fargo had been thinking about the same thing. "If we can get out of the mountains, there's a Mormon settlement off to the northeast. I don't know what sort of reception you'd get there, though. The Mormons usually don't care much for Gentiles. You can give it a try if you want. Chances are they wouldn't turn you away, even though they wouldn't be overly friendly."

"What about you, Skye?" Maureen asked. "Couldn't you stay there, too?"

Fargo shook his head. "If you try for it, I'll have to leave the train before you get there, and you'd do well not to mention my name. I've had some run-ins in the past with the Danites, the Mormon gunmen who run things down in Utah. Some of them might be up here, too."

"Well, if you can't go there, I don't think it's a good idea that we do," Maureen declared.

"We have to do what's best for all of us," Milo snapped.

"That's right," Fargo said before Maureen could argue with her former brother-in-law. "But we may be wasting our time talking about the whole thing. We can't reach Fort Hall *or* the Morman settlement without getting out of these mountains, and I'm pretty sure the pass to the south is blocked. No telling when it'll clear out enough to let the wagons through."

"You can't be sure of that," Milo pointed out.

Fargo nodded. "You're right. That's why I intend to ride down there and take a look as soon as I've had something to eat."

"Breakfast will be ready soon," Maureen said.

Fargo walked around the camp while he was waiting. The snow on the ground was almost a foot deep. The Ovaro wouldn't have any trouble traveling through the white, powdery stuff, and out in the open, the wagons would be able to negotiate it, too. The problem areas would be the pass and the narrower spots in the valley, where the wind would have piled up deep drifts during the night. Right here, things didn't look too bad, but

Fargo knew appearances were often deceiving, especially in the high country.

He wasn't too fond of the way the sky was beginning to look, either. More clouds were blowing in, and his earlier optimism was waning. That flat, gray, leaden sky might hold more snow. He had hoped that when morning came, the storm would be completely over. He wasn't convinced that was the case.

Maureen called him over to the fire for breakfast. Fargo hunkered next to the flames and ate a couple of strips of the salt jowl he had provided, along with a single hotcake, washing down the meager fare with coffee. That was enough to keep him going, he decided. He had lived through plenty of lean times in his life, and a little hunger was nothing new to him.

"You should eat more, Skye," Maureen urged, but he shook his head.

"I'm fine," he assured her. "I'll get some grain for my horse, and then we'll be on our way."

A short time later, he was ready to leave. "I ought to be back by the middle of the day," he said to Milo and Maureen as he stood by their wagon, holding the Ovaro's reins. "All of you stay put, and keep a couple of guards posted all the time. Warn them not to get trigger-happy, though. If any Shoshones come along, make sure they're not friendly before you do any shooting."

"Do you think the Indians will bother us?" Milo asked worriedly.

"I think they're probably all denned up in their lodges, wrapped in buffalo robes and trying to stay warm," Fargo said with a grin. "That's what I'd be doing right now if I was a Shoshone warrior. But the guards need to keep their eyes open, just in case."

Milo nodded. "I'll see to it."

Fargo swung up into the saddle and lifted a hand in farewell. "I'll be back," he promised.

Maureen waved to him as he rode off. Milo just stood there, a habitual scowl on his bearded face. Milo didn't like him, Fargo thought. That was all right; he wasn't overly fond of Milo, either. But as long as they could work together for the safety of the whole group, that was all that mattered. They didn't have to be friends.

Fargo rode south, the Ovaro easily breaking a trail through the snow. Within a few minutes, the twists and turns of the valley took him out of sight of the wagons. He kept the stallion moving at an easy pace, not hurrying but not wasting any time, either. He thought Maureen, Milo, and the others would be all right until he got back from checking the pass, but he didn't want to be gone any longer than he had to be, just in case more trouble descended on the mostly hapless group.

As he rode, Fargo considered the plight of the pilgrims and just how often such groups of emigrants ran into trouble on their way west. Entire wagon trains had been wiped out by Indians, outlaws, cyclones, floods, disease . . . If there was anything that could go wrong on such a journey, it usually did, sooner or later. Some of the pilgrims on the Oregon Trail and the other trails that led west were competent enough, but all too many had no idea how to take care of themselves and their families once they got more than a day's ride away from civilization.

And yet they kept coming. Over the past two and a half decades, tens of thousands of people had left the East and headed west, and probably each and every one of them had been convinced they would find paradise when they got where they were going. Too often, their little patch of paradise turned out to be a lonely grave beside the trail, and sometimes not even that much. Some of them wound up as nothing more than bleaching bones scattered by scavengers.

Fargo admired their courage but not their common sense. Yet he couldn't blame them for wanting something better out of life. He had been east on a few occasions, had walked the teeming streets of Philadelphia and New York. He wouldn't have been able to stand such a life, either. The crowds and the lack of space and clean air and open skies would have driven him mad.

No, he didn't blame the emigrants for heading west. He just wished so many of them didn't have to die in their attempt to reach the promised land.

He rode up to the pass around midmorning and reined in with a grim expression on his bearded face. Just as he feared, the snow had drifted deeply in the opening that led down to the plains. A foot of the white stuff in the open translated to seven or eight feet of it in the pass. This snow wasn't loose and powdery, either. The wind had packed it in tight. The drift was even higher at the other end of the pass. Men with shovels might be able to dig their way through it, but that would take days, maybe weeks. And if more snow fell soon, as seemed likely, the situation would get worse before it got better.

One slim chance remained. It was early enough in the season for the wind to turn to the south and blow enough warmth up off the Great Plains to melt the snow. If that happened, the wagon train could get out of the valley and make a run for Fort Hall. Otherwise, those pilgrims could be bottled up in here for the next four or five months, maybe longer.

Some of them would starve to death before then, Fargo thought. Others would die of exposure if they had to spend the winter in those wagons. The vehicles just weren't built to provide enough protection from a blizzard. The prospects looked pretty damned bleak for the emigrants, Fargo decided.

But not completely hopeless. Not yet. He reined the Ovaro around and heeled the stallion into a trot. The going was easier and faster now, since the big horse had already broken a trail through the snow. Fargo had to get back and tell them what he had found, even though the news was bad. Then they would have to decide what they were going to do.

A lot of lives would be riding on that decision.

3

Maureen's face fell as soon as she saw Fargo's expression when he rode up. "The pass is blocked, isn't it?" she asked as he dismounted.

He nodded. "Just as I expected."

Milo came up behind his former sister-in-law. "How bad is it?"

"Bad enough that digging out would be a mighty big chore." Fargo glanced at the gray sky. "And if it snows any more, it might not be possible at all."

"Then we'd better get down there and get started," Milo said without hesitation. He looked around at the other members of the party, who had gathered behind him and Maureen to hear what Fargo had to report. "What do the rest of you say? Do we try to dig out while we still can?"

A thin-faced woman with mousy brown hair and a perpetually tired expression spoke up. "Why can't we just stay here until the snow melts?"

"That may not be until next spring," Fargo told her. "And you can't spend the winter in your wagons."

"But it might melt sooner than that," the woman insisted. "You said so last night, didn't you?"

Fargo nodded. "It's possible. I'm afraid it's a gamble no matter what you decide to do. The only thing that's not an option is trying to stay right here all winter. If you do that, there's a good chance none of you will make it through."

"What do you think, Skye?" Maureen asked. "Can we dig out in time?"

Fargo shook his head. "In my opinion, no. I think it's going to snow again either later today or tonight, and then that pass will be blocked so that you'd need blasting powder to get through it. And even that might not work because an explosion would probably cause an avalanche that would just block it again."

"Well, if we can't stay here, and we can't get through the pass, where can we go?" Milo's voice bristled with irritation and impatience as he asked the question.

"I've been thinking about that," Fargo said slowly. "I've heard stories about an old trappers' fort somewhere up here in this area. Nobody has used it for a long time, but those old mountain men built pretty sturdy shelters. If we could find that fort, you might be able to hole up there for a while, at least until the snow in the pass melts—if it does."

"And if it doesn't?" Milo snapped.

"Then at least you'd have a better place to try to wait out the winter."

Milo scowled. "What you mean is, we'd starve to death instead of freezing to death."

Fargo answered the glare with a cool stare of his own. "I'm not saying it would be easy. But you have some supplies to start with, and there are moose and elk up here. Moose steaks aren't the most appetizing fare, but a fella can live for a long time on them."

"And how do you figure we're going to kill a moose?" Milo demanded. "Throw rocks at it?"

"We have the two rifles and a pretty good supply of ammunition. Again, it'll be stretching things pretty thin if we have to stay there all winter, but we can make it if everyone pitches in and cooperates."

"I still say we should try to dig out. You don't even know if you can find that old fort."

"Won't know until I try," Fargo said. "If you want to try digging out, you're welcome to." He looked at the others. "I can't make the decision for you folks. But as for myself, I'm going to ride on up the valley and see if I can find that fort."

The problem hung there in the air, and the emigrants clearly were uncomfortable as they tried to decide what to do. Fargo understood that they didn't want to go against Milo, who was the nominal leader. But so far, Milo hadn't performed too well in that role, and some of the group probably didn't trust him anymore. On the other hand, Fargo wasn't offering them any guarantees, either. They were between a rock and a hard place, and whichever way they turned, they might be facing death.

Finally, a tall, rawboned man with a slight Swedish accent spoke up. "I say we stay here while Mr. Fargo goes and looks for that fort. He seems to know what he's doing, *ja?*"

"I reckon that sounds all right to me," another man agreed. "If Fargo can't find the fort, we can still try to dig out later."

"But he said it would be impossible to do that if it snows more!" Milo exclaimed.

"I still think we should do like Mr. Fargo says," the Swede said.

This wasn't going well, Fargo thought. Milo Haydon had drawn a line and put himself on the opposite side of it. Fargo didn't want to take over the bunch and make an enemy out of Milo. But he couldn't just sit by and not offer them what seemed like their best option, either.

"All right," Milo said after a moment. His mouth twisted in bitter anger. "We'll do what he says. After all, he's the Trailsman." Scorn practically dripped from Milo's words.

Fargo reined in some anger of his own. Milo would come around, he told himself. It was better just to let things go for now.

"As soon as my horse has rested a little longer, I'll head on up the valley," Fargo said.

"Do you want something to eat before you go?" Maureen asked.

Fargo shook his head. "I've got some jerky in my saddlebags," he said. "That'll do me." He wasn't going to use any of the group's provisions if he didn't have to. They might need every scrap of food they had before they got out of this mess.

Milo stomped off, muttering to himself. The rest of the emigrants crowded around Fargo, introducing themselves and offering him encouragement in his effort to find the old fort. Fargo made himself smile and speak pleasantly to them, but he had to wonder how many of them would still be alive come spring if they were forced to spend the winter up here. He remembered hearing about what had happened to a party of emigrants who were trapped in the high mountains of California back in '46. Only a few had survived, and in the end they had been reduced to eating the bodies of their less fortunate companions. His jaw tightened as he looked at Maureen and at the children running around the camp, playing in the snow. He would do everything in his power to see to it that such a grisly fate didn't await them.

A short time later, when he was getting the Ovaro ready to go, he was startled to see Maureen coming toward him, leading a saddled horse. She was wearing gloves, a heavy coat, and a floppy-brimmed felt hat. "What do you think you're doing?" Fargo asked.

"Going with you, of course," she replied.

Fargo shook his head. "You need to stay here with the others. I can't be watching out for you and looking for that fort at the same time." He didn't mean to be deliberately harsh, but he wasn't going to sugarcoat the facts, either.

"You won't have to watch out for me," Maureen said. "I'm perfectly capable of looking out for myself. I've been riding since I was a little girl." Her gloved hand patted the shoulder of the chestnut gelding she had led up. "And this is a fine horse. We used to ride into town from the farm all the time."

"Illinois farm roads are a lot different from mountain trails," Fargo said. "And I'll be setting a pretty fast pace."

"If we can't keep up, we'll turn around and come back."

"Not by yourself. I'd have to turn around and bring you back."

Anger flared in her dark brown eyes. "Damn it, Skye! I'm telling you I can do this. I want to help. And I . . . I want to be with you."

Fargo frowned. He wasn't sure what Maureen had in mind, but he could make a pretty good guess, he decided. As pleasant as that prospect was, he couldn't see risking both their lives for a little privacy so they could explore their mutual desires. He was about to say as much—discreetly, of course—when Maureen sighed and said, "Milo told me you wouldn't let me go. He said I was just wasting my time."

Fargo's eyes narrowed. He stared at her for a moment, then gave an abrupt laugh. "You didn't really think that old trick was going to work, did you?"

Maureen blew her breath out in exasperation, causing a cloud of steam to form in front of her face. "I thought it might be worth a try."

Fargo shook his head. "I'm not going to risk your life just to annoy Milo."

"How about this, then?" Maureen gave him a bold, defiant look. "Take me with you or I'll just follow you anyway."

"You'd do that even if I told you not to?"

"Now who's being foolish?" she shot back at him.

They traded intense stares for a long moment, and finally Fargo sighed. "All right," he said. "But if you can't keep up, you *will* have to come back by yourself. I won't waste the time to bring you back." He wasn't sure if he meant the threat or not. He supposed they would both have to wait and see, and if they were lucky, the situation wouldn't come up.

He swung up into the Ovaro's saddle, and Maureen mounted the chestnut. Her skirt was split, and she rode astride, Fargo saw. That raised her a notch in his estimation. No sidesaddle gal could have hoped to make the trek through these rugged mountains.

Milo strode up before Fargo and Maureen rode off.

He glared at both of them and said to her, "My God, you're really going to do it."

"It makes sense, Milo," she said. "This way, if we find the fort, there's twice as much chance that one of us will get back here with the information."

"You really think if something happens to Fargo that you'd be able to make it back on your own?" Milo's derisive tone made it clear how unlikely he considered that possibility.

"You just hide and watch," Maureen snapped. She reined her horse around and heeled it into motion, taking off up the valley at a fast walk.

Fargo couldn't resist lifting a finger to the brim of his hat and giving Milo a grin as he turned the Ovaro to ride after Maureen.

But he might not have done it if Milo had a gun right then, he told himself, still grinning. Might have been a good way to get shot in the back.

Fargo had to admit that Maureen rode well, and the chestnut seemed to have plenty of strength and stamina. There was no telling how long that would last, though, in either woman or horse. Only time would tell.

The Big Lost River bubbled and chuckled along beside them, its current fast. In a few more weeks, it would be frozen over, but for now the thick layer of ice to come had not yet formed on its surface. The pine-covered mountain slopes rose sharply to the right and left of the two riders. In places, the angle was almost perpendicular. The twisting path between the mountains was more a canyon than a valley.

"No wonder no one ever settled up here," Maureen said. "There's hardly any level ground."

"Not like Illinois, eh?"

"Have you ever been there?"

Fargo nodded. "Ridden through a time or two. Never stayed for any amount of time, though."

"I get the feeling that's something you can say about most places."

Fargo laughed. "That's just about right." He lifted a hand and pointed ahead of them. "The valley widens out in a few more miles. It's still not any place you'd want to settle down and start a farm, but the quarters aren't as cramped as they are along here."

"Do you think that's where the fort is?"

"More than likely," Fargo said. "If it's even up here."

She looked over at him. "You're not sure it's even there, are you?"

"Not completely. I've been thinking about it all day. I know I remember hearing stories about an old fort up here in one of these valleys, and I *think* it was this one. But I don't know for sure."

Maureen was silent for a moment, then she said, "If it's not there, then we're all going to die, aren't we? Or most of us, anyway."

"Not necessarily," Fargo told her.

"But if it starts to snow again—"

"It already is," Fargo said. He pointed. "Look."

A snowflake floated down in front of the horses. A few seconds later, another followed, then more and more. At first they were fairly small, but they grew larger as they continued to fall at a faster and faster rate. Maureen gave a hollow laugh. "It's beautiful," she said. "Or at least it would be if it didn't mean that our chances of getting out of here are dwindling away with every flake that falls."

Fargo estimated that they had come several miles since leaving the camp, and the pass was still several miles ahead. "Maybe it's not snowing at the pass," he said, although a glance at the sky told him the developing snowstorm was pretty widespread.

"You know better, Skye."

"I know I'm not one to give up," Fargo said. "I don't reckon you should, either."

"You're right." She forced a smile. "Let's go find that fort."

Fargo picked up the pace. They rode on, and as he had told Maureen earlier, within a short time the valley began to widen. The distance between the mountain ranges grew larger, until more than a mile separated them. Despite its name, the river ran closer to the Sawtooths on the west than it did to the Lost River Mountains on the east. The towering peaks that closed off the valley's upper end were visible ahead, though the swirling snow hid them part of the time. Thick stands of pine and spruce bordered some open, parklike areas. In the spring and summer, these high mountain meadows were beautiful, Fargo knew, covered with lush green grass and brilliantly colored wildflowers. But the ground was too rocky for farming and there wasn't enough graze to raise cattle or horses. Maybe someday civilization would make its way here, but for now this country belonged to the moose and the elk, the eagle and the beaver, the chipmunk and the otter. Man had no place here.

But that had not always been true, and as Fargo reined in, he saw the evidence up ahead. His heart gave a little leap as he pointed. "There," he told Maureen. "Some of the stockade wall is still standing."

She brought her horse to a halt and looked where he was pointing. "My God," she breathed. "It's really there."

Some two hundred yards ahead of them, on a small hill that rose on the far side of a little depression, stood a ten-foot-tall wall made of peeled and sharpened pine logs. It seemed to be mostly intact, though some of the logs had fallen. The stockade was three hundred feet long and about that deep. Fargo couldn't see inside the wall, but he suspected there were several cabins inside the fort, as well as a larger building that the trappers would have used as a warehouse for their furs. The structures were probably in various states of disrepair, but they could be fixed up. Even the way they were now, they were a big improvement over trying to spend the winter in a bunch of canvas-covered wagons.

"Let's go take a look," Fargo said. He heeled the Ovaro into a trot.

They rode toward the abandoned fort, Maureen still keeping pace easily. Fargo slowed the stallion to a walk as they neared the gates, which hung askew on leather hinges that were partially rotten. He flexed his fingers and then moved his hand closer to the Colt on his hip. "Stay behind me for a minute," he said to Maureen.

"Why? What's wrong, Skye?"

"Nothing. I just don't believe in taking chances, that's all. And barging into a place unannounced is running a risk out here."

"But I thought you said this fort was abandoned."

"As far as I know, it is." Fargo glanced over at Maureen. "But just in case it's not . . ."

She swallowed and nodded, then slowed down and moved her horse over so that she was behind Fargo, as he had requested.

A minute later, when he was about fifty feet from the gates, he brought the stallion to a stop and rested his hand on the butt of the Colt. "Hello, the fort!" he called, his deep voice ringing out with enough power to carry to the far corners of the stockade. "Anybody home? We're not looking for trouble, just a place to get in out of the weather!"

Silence was the only response from the fort. The wind, not nearly as hard today as it had been the night before, soughed softly in the branches of the pines.

"Hello!" Fargo called again. There was still no answer. He turned and nodded to Maureen. "Reckon we can go in now."

A part of his mind remained unconvinced and still halfway expected somebody to take a shot at the two of them. But they rode through the gap between the gates and into the fort without anything happening. The place was still quiet and peaceful. Fargo reined in, leaned forward in the saddle, and looked around.

As he had suspected, there had been several buildings inside the fort, all of them built of logs. A couple were in ruins, with roofs that had fallen in and walls that were partially collapsed. One cabin had been burned, leaving only a few charred remains that had been mostly overgrown by vegetation. But half a dozen of the cabins were still standing, Fargo saw, as was the larger building that had been the fur warehouse. That was a stroke of luck.

Several families could share it. Once some repairs were made, there would be enough shelter here for everyone in the wagon train.

Food was a different story, but first things first, Fargo told himself. People froze to death a lot faster than they starved, so getting out of the weather was the most important priority now. The river was close by, and if the pilgrims had to ride out the winter here, they could chop through the ice for water or even melt some of the snow. With luck, they could bring down enough game to feed themselves. It would be a lean and hungry time, Fargo thought, but they could do it. They could survive.

Of course, it would be a hell of a lot better if one more warm spell came along and melted the snow in that pass. Fargo was going to keep hoping for that, but in case it didn't happen, the emigrants would have to be prepared to wait for spring.

Fargo swung down from the saddle. "I'm going to check out some of those cabins," he told Maureen.

"I'll come with you," she said as she hurriedly dismounted. Fargo could tell that she didn't want to be separated from him, but he didn't take it as a compliment. There was something vaguely disquieting about the abandoned fort. Fargo wasn't surprised to be feeling that sensation. He had been in other places that once had been full of life, only to be left behind, empty and deserted. Some people might say it was like the spirits of the former occupants lingered around such places. Fargo wasn't a superstitious man, but he had seen enough strange things in his wanderings that he didn't discount many possibilities. No matter how creepy the old fort was, though, he was mighty glad to have found the place.

He looked inside one of the cabins and found it pretty much intact. There was a hole in the roof that needed patching, but that wouldn't be any trouble. In the next cabin he checked, several gaps between the logs in the walls would have to be chinked with mud, but again, that wasn't a problem. One by one he examined the buildings and found that all of them would be livable with a little work. After the events of the past twenty-four hours, things finally were looking up for the pilgrims from back east.

"Skye," Maureen said, and Fargo thought he heard a trace of worry in her voice. "Can we get back to the wagons before it gets dark?"

Fargo looked up at the sky for a moment and then shook his head. "I don't think so. If it wasn't so cloudy, we might have made it, but I'm afraid we'd lose the light before we got back if we started now."

"Then we'll have to stay . . . here . . . tonight?"

He nodded. "We'll leave first thing in the morning. By tomorrow night the wagons will be here, and we can get started making it a fit place to live for a while."

"Not too long, I hope." Maureen smiled, but her eyes still looked worried. "There's something about it that just . . . makes me uncomfortable."

"I know what you mean," Fargo agreed. "But there's nothing here except maybe a few mice." He started toward the warehouse building, which was the only one he hadn't looked at yet. "Come on."

The hinges on the building's single big door were in better shape than those on the gates. The door was closed properly. Fargo grasped the rope handle on it and pulled. The door swung toward him, and a distinctive smell rolled out of the building.

The smell of something dead.

"Oh, my God!" Maureen said. "What's that?"

Fargo slipped his revolver from its holster. "I don't know," he murmured as he narrowed his eyes and tried to peer into the shadowy interior of the building. The gloom was too thick for him to see much. He could make out the high ceiling and a few feet of hard-packed earthen floor, but that was about all.

Maureen clutched at his arm as he started forward. "Skye, don't go in there!" she said a voice that was ragged with fear.

"Whatever's in there, it's dead," Fargo told her. "But I want to take a look around anyway. Stay here." Gently, he pried his arm out of her grip.

Maureen watched anxiously as Fargo stepped into the warehouse. His eyes began to adjust to the gloom almost immediately. He saw a large dark heap on the floor in front of him. A dead bear, he wondered? But a bear couldn't have closed the door behind itself. And why would a bear go into a building to die in the first place?

Fargo reached out with a booted foot and prodded the heap on the floor. It gave under his touch. He knelt down and put out his free hand, felt bristly fur and knew what he had found. He straightened with a chuckle and called over his shoulder to Maureen, "It's a pile of buffalo robes, that's all."

"Thank goodness. Is that what the smell's coming from?"

Fargo walked around the rest of the cavernous warehouse. "There are probably some dead rats or mice in here somewhere," he said. "The place is empty other than that. We'll leave the door open for a while and let it air out. Can't get any colder in here than it already is."

The temperature was dropping, and that concerned him. He and Maureen would have to build a fire in one of the cabins. They all had fireplaces, so if he could find one where the chimney wasn't clogged, that wouldn't be a problem. He holstered his gun, and as he walked back toward the entrance, he bent over and took hold of one of the buffalo robes. Dragging it behind him, he went outside.

Maureen wrinkled her nose. "You don't intend to use that, do you?"

"I'll throw it over a tree limb for a while. By nightfall it won't smell so bad. And it'll feel mighty good tonight if the temperature keeps dropping."

Over the next hour, Fargo picked out the cabin that was in the best shape. He left the stockade long enough to go out and gather an armload of broken branches from underneath the nearby pines. He wanted enough wood to keep a fire going all night, so that he wouldn't have to go out and hunt for more in the dark. By the time he had a merry little blaze going in the fireplace, the light outside was beginning to fade. He brought in the buffalo robe and spread it on the dirt floor in front of the fire.

"You're right," Maureen said. "I guess it doesn't smell too bad."

Fargo grinned at her. "Have a seat. I'll tend to the horses, and then we can have supper."

Supper would be strips of jerky, the same as lunch had been, only they wouldn't have to eat in the saddle this time. Fargo led the horses into the warehouse building where they would be out of the wind, unsaddled them, took off the wet blankets and replaced them with dry ones from his pack. He gave them both some grain from the supply he carried for the Ovaro, cupping a small amount in the palm of his hand so that each horse could eat.

When the horses were settled for the night, Fargo slung his saddlebags over his shoulder and went back to the cabin where he had left Maureen. To keep as much snow and cold air out as possible, he ducked quickly through the door and swung it shut behind him.

When he turned toward the fireplace, he stopped short. Maureen was sitting on the buffalo robe, all right, but she had pulled it up around her. Her bare shoulders were visible above the robe, and Fargo wondered if the rest of her was equally bare. He had a hunch that he would find out before too much longer.

"I warned you," she said with a smile. "I'm feeling downright brazen these days."

Fargo set the saddlebags aside. Supper could wait.

4

Maureen was nude under the buffalo robe, just as Fargo suspected. She let the robe slip lower as he approached. The fire hadn't been burning for very long, and it was still rather cold in the cabin. Goose bumps stood out on Maureen's fair skin. She lowered the robe a little more, and Fargo saw her nipples. They were so hard they stood out a good half inch. He didn't know if that reaction was from the cold, or the passion she was feeling. Probably a little bit of both, he thought. He would just have to warm them up and see for himself.

He knelt in front of her and took off his hat, tossing it to one side. Lowering his head, he fastened his lips over the pebbled crown of her left breast. Maureen sighed as Fargo ran his tongue around the nipple and then sucked gently on it. "That feels so good, Skye," she said.

"And we're just getting started," he told her as he lifted his mouth from her breast. He moved over and suckled the other nipple for a moment while he used his right hand to cup and knead her left breast. When he raised his head this time, she put a hand behind his neck and pulled him toward her. Their mouths met in a kiss that seemed even hotter to Fargo than the waves of heat coming from the fireplace.

His tongue tasted her lips. They opened easily under the probing caress. He explored her mouth, reveling in the hot sweetness of it. At the same time, he filled both hands with her breasts and strummed her nipples with his thumbs. She reached inside his coat and caught at his chest, bunching the buckskin shirt in her hands.

"Oh, Skye," she murmured when they finally broke the kiss. "I need you now. I can't wait."

"I won't make you wait," Fargo promised.

He pulled off his boots and stripped out of the sheepskin coat and buckskin shirt and trousers. Maureen's eager fingers took hold of the long underwear he wore and peeled them down over his hips. His erect shaft bobbed up as she freed it from its confinement. Maureen sighed as she closed her hand around the thick pole of male flesh.

"I want you inside me, Skye." She lay back, letting the buffalo robe fall to the sides around her. Her legs parted, thighs spreading wide to reveal the thick triangle of dark brown hair that covered her mound and the folds of flesh below it. She was still gripping his organ, and Fargo knew she was anxious for him to make love to her, but he paused long enough to rest his hand on her mound and rub it for a moment. Maureen cried out in pleasure.

Then Fargo moved over her, poised to enter her. She brought the head of his shaft to her already drenched opening. As he felt the wet heat begin to engulf the tip, his hips surged forward slowly. He buried himself within her, sheathing every last inch of his manhood inside her clasping core. Maureen uttered a long cry of passion as he penetrated her.

"Yes, yes!" She panted as Fargo launched into the timeless rhythm of man and woman joining together. "Give it to me, Skye! Give me everything you've got!"

Fargo did as she asked, driving as deeply inside her as he could with each stroke and then withdrawing until he was almost out before surging forward again. Maureen wrapped her legs around him and locked her ankles together above his pistoning hips. Her arms went around his neck and pulled him down so that she could kiss him again. This time her tongue went slithering urgently into his mouth as her full breasts flattened under his broad, muscular chest. Fargo felt his own passion, his own need for release, growing stronger as he stroked harder and faster into her. She matched him thrust for thrust, her hips bucking up against his.

Fargo knew he wouldn't be able to hold off much longer. From the way Maureen was gasping and panting against his mouth, he figured she wouldn't be able to, either. They had all night, he reminded himself. They could do this again and again, exploring every inch of each other's bodies and making love as many times as humanly possible. He couldn't think of a better way to spend a snowy night in the high country.

As it inevitably must, the culmination of their love-making came to an end. Fargo nuzzled Maureen's neck, then tightened his arms around her. With his shaft still buried inside her, he rolled over on the buffalo robe so that he was on the bottom and she was resting atop him. She put her head on his shoulder and sighed. He could feel her heart hammering solidly against his chest and supposed that she could feel his as well.

"That was so wonderful, Skye," she whispered. "I needed it so much. I can't thank you—"

"You don't have to thank me," Fargo broke into her declaration. "I reckon we both got what we needed."

"This time." Maureen laughed. "But what if I need it again later?"

"I'll do my best to oblige," Fargo answered with a grin.

He was awake first the next morning and slipped out of the buffalo robe without waking Maureen. The fire had died down until it was just glowing embers. Fargo's breath fogged in front of his face as he quickly pulled on his clothes and boots. He knelt in front of the fireplace and bent over to blow on the coals to make them glow a brighter red. He slowly fed in wood shavings and watched them catch fire. As the flames grew stronger, he added more wood until he had a small but friendly blaze going.

Fargo stood up and turned to watch Maureen sleeping. Her hair was tousled around her face. Her eyes were closed, and she looked peaceful and somehow younger. One hand stuck out from under the robe. Though it showed signs of hard work, the fingers were still slender and graceful. Maureen had suffered tragedy and hardship in her life, but she hadn't allowed any of it to make her bitter. She was still a vital, hopeful young woman.

Fargo buckled on his gunbelt. He would have felt a little better if he'd had his Henry rifle with him, too, but it had been more important to leave it for the guards at the wagon train. If he ran into trouble that he couldn't stop with the heavy revolver on his hip, it wasn't likely that he could have done much better with the rifle. Both weapons were the same caliber; the rifle just had a much longer range and held more shots.

After putting on his hat and coat, Fargo went to the door of the cabin. He pulled it open and stepped outside. The wind had died down again during the night. Fargo tipped his head back and looked at the sky. The sun wasn't up yet, but there was enough gray illumination from the approaching dawn that he could tell the overcast remained. A few stray snowflakes came down, adding to the foot and a half already on the ground. The storm had hit a lull, but it wasn't over yet. This was a big one for the time of year, Fargo thought. It had lasted more than thirty-six hours so far, with still more to come. It was looking more likely with each passing moment that the group of pilgrims would not be able to get out of the valley before spring.

In that case, they would just have to settle in here for the winter. At least they would have a chance to do so and maybe make it through.

Shivering inside his sheepskin coat, Fargo headed for the warehouse building to check on the horses. The stallion whinnied a greeting when he came in, and Fargo grinned and patted the big horse on the shoulder. Maureen's chestnut seemed glad to see him, too. It was dim and shadowy inside the building, even with the door open. Fargo saddled the horses and led them outside. With both sets of reins in his hand, he walked out through the stockade gates and down to the river to let the horses drink. They plunged their muzzles into the icy-cold stream. Fargo filled his canteen and took a long swallow from it. The water was so frigid it almost took his breath away, but it tasted good.

When he got back to the gate with the horses, he saw a few tendrils of smoke wisping up from the chimney of the cabin where he and Maureen had spent the night. He wondered if she was awake yet.

A second later, he got his answer—in the form of a terrified scream.

The thick walls of the cabin muffled the sound, but Fargo clearly heard the shriek anyway. He dropped the reins as both horses shied back nervously. The screaming might have spooked the chestnut, but not the Ovaro, Fargo thought as he reached for his gun and ran toward the cabin. The big black-and-white stallion could stay calm in the middle of a roaring gunfight. If the Ovaro was upset, it was because he had smelled or otherwise sensed something that he really didn't like.

Those thoughts raced through Fargo's mind as he sprinted toward the cabin. He didn't call out; if somebody or something was after Maureen, he didn't want to give the attacker any warning that help was on the way. He burst through the door with the Colt leveled, his arm swinging from side to side as his keen eyes searched for a target.

Fargo didn't see anything threatening. His gaze darted to the corners of the cabin's single room. Maureen was huddled in a rear corner, well away from the fireplace. She had the buffalo robe clutched tightly around her, and her eyes were wide and staring in terror. At first she didn't seem to recognize Fargo, but then she cried out, "Skye!" and came to her feet. She practically threw herself into his arms. He kept the gun ready in his right hand but tightened his left arm around her. He could feel the way she was trembling even through the thick buffalo robe.

"What is it?" he asked sharply. "What's wrong, Maureen?"

She didn't answer right away, just pressed her face against his chest and sniffled. Fargo finished looking around the room. It was empty except for the two of them. He wondered if Maureen had had a nightmare. Fargo had never been the sort to be plagued by such things, but he knew some people had dreams that were so bad, they woke up screaming.

"What happened?" he asked, his tone more gentle now. "Did something scare you, Maureen?"

She lifted her head so that he could see her face. Her cheeks were streaked with tears. "That . . . that thing!" she exclaimed. "It was some sort of . . . of monster!"

Fargo was convinced now that she'd had a nightmare. There were no monsters in this old, abandoned fort. But he didn't want to offend her by telling her bluntly that she was just imagining things, so he said, "What did it look like?"

She clutched at his chest and choked back sobs of fear. "It . . . it was huge. I've never seen anything like it. I thought at first it . . . it might be a bear. It was standing by the fireplace when I woke up. But then . . . it turned around . . . and I saw its face . . . that awful face . . ." She started to cry again and couldn't talk anymore.

Fargo holstered his gun, satisfied there was no real threat here. He held Maureen in both arms for a moment, stroking her hair in a calming gesture. Gradually she stopped crying.

"What was it, Skye?" she asked when she could speak again. "What could that thing have been?"

"I don't know," Fargo replied. "You say you had just woke up when you saw it?"

"Yes, I—" She stopped short and frowned at him. "What do you mean by that question?"

"I'm just trying to figure out—"

"If I've gone mad?" she broke in. "Or if I just dreamed it? Is that what you mean, Skye? You think I can't tell the difference between a dream and something that's real?"

"That's not what I'm saying," Fargo told her. "Sometimes folks are a mite confused when they first wake up, though."

"I'm not confused!" Her body was taut with anger now, but she didn't try to pull away from him. "I know what I saw. That thing was in here. It . . . it came over and bent down to look at me . . . " She shuddered again and lifted her hands to press them over her face. "Oh, God, it was terrible. It was like nothing human. I thought . . . I thought it was going to kill me . . ."

"It was shaggy, like a bear, but it didn't have a bear's face?"

"That's right. I've never seen anything like it. I . . . I can't even begin to describe how awful it was."

"Then what I can't figure out," Fargo said, "is where the blamed thing went."

"What?" Maureen frowned again and shook her head in confusion. "I don't understand."

"Look around the room," Fargo told her. "Where did it go?"

Maureen did as he told her, turning her head to examine the room. Her eyes, red-rimmed from crying, widened as she did so. The room was empty. The only way in or out was by the door; there were no windows.

"It must have run out the door," she murmured.

Fargo shook his head. "I was looking right at the cabin when I heard you scream the first time. Nothing came out the door. I would have seen it if it did."

"You were startled," Maureen said. "You might not have noticed—No, that's foolish, isn't it? The thing was huge. If it went out the door, you couldn't have missed it."

"Come over here and take a look," Fargo said, drawing her toward the still-open door. "The floor in here is too hard-packed to take any tracks, but look at the snow outside." He pointed. "You can see my tracks where I went out, and those are from when I ran back over here. You can see for yourself that there aren't any more footprints."

"No, there aren't," Maureen said. "But, Skye, I know what I saw—"

45

"You couldn't have. There's no place for anybody—or anything—to have gone."

After a moment, she sighed. "You're right. I'm being foolish to insist on it, aren't I?"

Fargo shrugged. "I reckon you believed you saw something. I don't doubt that for a second."

"But why . . . why would I have such a bizarre dream?"

"I can't tell you that."

"And it seemed so real," Maureen insisted.

"Most dreams usually do," Fargo said.

"That's true, of course." Maureen studied the marks in the snow again. "I have to accept what you're telling me. There's the proof, right there. The only other explanation is if the monster vanished into thin air, and I can't believe that."

"Neither can I." Fargo smiled at her and changed the subject by saying, "You'd better get dressed. We've got to get back on the trail pretty soon if we want to reach the wagons and bring them back here by nightfall."

"Yes. That's right." Maureen summoned up a smile, but it was considerably weaker than Fargo's. "The storm isn't over yet, is it?"

"Doesn't look like it," Fargo agreed. "As far as the weather's concerned, I figure it's going to get worse before it gets better."

That worried him, and so did the Ovaro's reaction when Maureen had screamed. He hadn't told her about that, because he really didn't know what to make of it. It seemed unlikely to him that the stallion would have reacted like that simply because of a scream. Fargo didn't have an answer to that question, but he wasn't ready to believe in monsters. Not without seeing some proof with his own eyes.

Their breakfast was a fast one, and as soon as they were finished, they mounted up and headed back down the valley. The tracks their horses had made in the snow the day before were covered up now by the new snow that had fallen during the night. The Ovaro and the chestnut had to break a path again. That was tiring work for the animals, and Fargo called a halt fairly often to let the horses rest.

Maureen was quiet, and Fargo figured she was thinking about what had happened that morning. That was a shame, because he'd rather she were thinking about the things they had done together the night before, as well as the things they would do in the future, if they got a chance. More than likely, they would have those chances, because Fargo intended to stay with the emigrants until they reached safety. He had no doubt that, traveling alone, he could make it out of the mountains once the storm was over, whether the pass was blocked or not. But he wasn't going to do that if it meant leaving these greenhorns to fend for themselves. He wouldn't be able to live with himself if he knew he had ridden away when he could have stayed and helped.

Around midmorning, Maureen gave a small, forced laugh. "You really must have thought I'd lost my mind this morning, Skye," she said. "I appreciate you not saying so."

"Not at all," Fargo told her. "Anybody can be mistaken about something."

"It just seemed so real," Maureen mused, then she stopped and gave a shake of her head. "No, I'm not going to start thinking about it again. There's no point in it."

Fargo didn't argue with her.

The valley soon narrowed down again. The dark slopes seemed to loom ominously above them as they rode. Fargo sternly told himself not to let his imagination run away with him. He had traveled through valleys just like this many times in the past. There was nothing strange about it, no reason for him to think that anything was out of the ordinary.

But he couldn't quite forget the way the Ovaro had acted, shying away in the gray dawn like he had scented something wild, something evil . . .

"We ought to be back before too much longer," Maureen said, breaking into Fargo's thoughts.

He nodded. "Yep. I hope your brother-in-law has everybody ready to travel."

"You don't like Milo very much, do you?"

The blunt question took Fargo a little by surprise. "I reckon I'm about as fond of him as he is of me."

"I know he's rather gruff, but he's a good man."

"I don't doubt it."

"He took care of everything when Daniel died. I never would have made it without his help."

"Maybe he blames himself for what happened. He said he was with your husband when those floodwaters swept him away." Fargo didn't want to hurt Maureen with those old, painful memories, but she was the one who had brought it up.

"You're probably right. They were very close, of course, being brothers."

"It's natural Milo would look out for you," Fargo said. "Maybe the reason he and I didn't hit it off is because he could tell how much I admired you."

Maureen stared over at Fargo for a moment as she rode alongside him, then she laughed. "Are you saying that Milo is *jealous?* I can't believe that."

"He's fond of you, anybody can see that. And he's not really your brother-in-law anymore."

"No, but still . . . I just can't believe that, Skye. Milo has always been a perfect gentleman around me."

"Well, it could be I'm wrong," Fargo said, but the more he thought about it, the more likely the explanation seemed. Milo was older than Maureen, but not by much. And there was a bond between them starting out, because of Maureen's marriage to Daniel. Fargo didn't think it was impossible at all for Milo to harbor hopes of someday replacing his late brother in Maureen's affections.

A little later, they came within sight of the wagons. Fargo saw smoke from the fires before he saw the actual wagons. But then the big canvas-covered vehicles appeared. Someone sang out to let the emigrants know that Fargo and Maureen were coming. By the time they reined their mounts to a halt beside Maureen's wagon, the whole company had assembled. Milo Haydon stepped out in front of the others and said fervently, "Thank God you're all right. When you didn't get back last night, we were all afraid the storm had gotten you or something else terrible had happened."

"We ran out of time to get back before nightfall," Fargo explained. "So we spent the night at the old fort."

Something flickered in Milo's eyes at the mention of Fargo and Maureen spending the night together, and Fargo was more convinced than ever that he was right about the way Milo felt about her. But Milo only said, "Then the fort's there, like you thought?"

Fargo nodded. "It's a little run-down, but the buildings are pretty solid. If we get the wagons moving without any delay, we can get there not long after dark."

"That's good to hear," one of the other men said. "It got mighty cold in these here wagons last night, Mr. Fargo, let me tell you."

"You'll all be warmer tonight," Fargo promised.

Everyone got busy preparing to leave. Teams were hitched to the wagons, goods that had been taken out were loaded again, and fires were put out, though in this weather with snow covering the ground there was no danger of a blaze spreading. Fargo would have liked to give the stallion more rest, but there wasn't time. As things stood now, it would take all afternoon, at the very least, to reach the abandoned fort, and, as Fargo had told the group, it probably would be after dark before they arrived.

The guard who had been carrying Fargo's Henry rifle brought the weapon back to him. "Here you go, Mr. Fargo," the young man said. "I'm obliged for the loan of the rifle. It's a mighty nice gun."

Fargo nodded. "You didn't have any trouble while I was gone?"

"Naw, ever'thing was quiet." The young man cast a glance toward Milo's wagon and dropped his voice so that no one would overhear. "Except for Mr. Haydon stompin' around and growlin' like an old bear. He sure was mad about you bein' gone all night with Miss Maureen."

"It couldn't be helped," Fargo said. He wondered if Milo suspected what had happened between them while they were at the fort. Given what was evidently a suspicious nature on Milo's part, Fargo figured it was pretty likely.

The wagons were rolling less than an hour after Fargo and Maureen got back. Fargo took the lead. Milo's wagon was the first in line, followed by Maureen's with the others trailing behind. Maureen's saddle horse was tied to the back of her wagon, and she handled her own team of oxen. When Fargo offered to help, she smiled at him and said, "I've driven these brutes hundreds of miles already, Skye. I think I can manage a few more."

The clouds still blotted out the sun, but so far during the day, only a few flakes of snow had fallen. Fargo hoped the snow would hold off until they reached the fort. The animals and the wagons had enough trouble dealing with what was already on the ground. The pace was slow but steady, and the trail he and Maureen had broken that morning was still easy to follow. The light changed subtly as the afternoon advanced, becoming more and more gray. Darkness slipped in almost unnoticed.

Fargo kept moving, trusting to his keen sense of direction to guide him even though it was hard to see much after a while. When he turned in the saddle and looked behind him, he could barely make out the lead wagon. He had warned the drivers to stay close together once it got dark, so they wouldn't get separated. Anyone who took a wrong turn and wandered off likely would never be found until it was too late.

Instinct told Fargo that the valley had opened up around them. He kept the sound of the river on his right hand and forged ahead. When the Ovaro started down a gentle slope, he knew he had reached the shallow depression in front of the fort. He rode ahead until he could make out a dark line against the snow that he recognized as the stockade fence. Turning, he headed back to the wagons.

"Keep moving straight ahead!" he called to Milo Haydon when he reached the lead wagon. "It's not more than two hundred yards to the fort!"

Milo waved a hand in acknowledgement. Fargo rode on, and when he reached Maureen's wagon and told her they were almost at their destination, she exclaimed, "Thank God! I thought we'd never get here, Skye."

"Just keep going," he said. "Don't lose sight of Milo's wagon."

He moved along the wagon train, counting each vehicle one by one as he passed the word that they were almost there. A feeling of relief went through him when he reached the end of the line and realized that all the wagons were accounted for. He hadn't lost anyone during the journey. Wheeling the Ovaro around, he trotted toward the front again and waved at Maureen as he passed her wagon. He even gave Milo a little wave, since he was feeling better about things now.

Fargo reined in at the gates, and without dismounting, he pulled them open even wider, giving the wagons plenty of room to pass through the fence. That done, he headed for the cabin where he and Maureen had spent the previous night. He intended to get a fire started in the fireplace there, then move on and get fires burning in some of the other cabins and the warehouse building. The warehouse didn't have a fireplace, but he could arrange a ring of stones in the center of the floor and use that as a makeshift fireplace. Later, a proper fire pit could be dug.

Fargo swung down from the saddle in front of the cabin. He was about to drop the Ovaro's reins, figuring he could leave the well-trained stallion ground-hitched, when he realized something was wrong. There was a new smell in the air tonight. It wasn't the smell of snow, or musty old buffalo robes, or dead mice. It was a smell that could mean only one thing.

Tobacco. Someone was inside the cabin.

As Fargo stiffened, he heard the muffled sound of a

horse's whinny and knew it came from inside the warehouse building. His hand started toward the butt of his Colt.

The door of the cabin swung open, and a harsh, high-pitched voice said, "Don't do it, friend. Just stand easy and keep your hand away from that hog leg, or sure as hell, I'll blow your damn head off!"

5

Fargo froze with his hand still inches away from the revolver, but his stance had nothing to do with the icy weather. He recognized the tone of menace in the words that had just been spoken and knew that whoever was in the cabin meant what he said.

Standing next to the stallion, Fargo said, "Take it easy, friend. I'm not looking for trouble, and neither are the folks with me."

Shadows moved in the doorway. The man who stepped out was medium-sized but appeared bigger because he wore a thick coat made from animal hide. It was too dark to make out much more than that. A faint red glow flared up, casting feeble illumination over a lean face that was mostly sharp angles. The man had a pipe clenched between his teeth and was puffing on it, which explained the smell of tobacco. He was also carrying something that Fargo took to be a shotgun.

"Who-all's out there?" the man asked. "Is that a bunch o' damn wagons I hear?"

"Some travelers have gotten stuck up here in the mountains and are looking for a place to get out of the weather," Fargo said. "The pass at the southern end of the valley is blocked."

The man snorted in disgust. "Well, o' course it's blocked! It's snowin', ain't it? Anyway, what's a bunch o' pilgrims doin' up here? This valley ain't on the way to anywhere they'd want to go."

"It's a long story. I can explain it all later. For right

now, I'd like to bring them on into the fort." As a matter of fact, the wagons were still rolling up to the stockade, and Milo would be at the gate in a matter of moments unless Fargo stopped him. He hoped that wouldn't be necessary.

The shadowy figure lowered the shotgun. "All right," he said grudgingly. "Don't reckon I can let anybody freeze to death, even a bunch o' damn greenhorns."

Fargo relaxed a little. "Thanks."

He had started to figure that this old-timer was probably one of the fur trappers who still worked their trade in these mountains. Many of the trappers went back east to the settlements to spend the winters, but some waited out the snow and ice up here so they could get a head start on collecting furs once the spring came. It wasn't really surprising that one of them was making use of the old fort.

"My name's Fargo," he went on.

The man grunted. "Ed Dugan. I'd say I'm glad to meet you, but then I'd be lyin'. I was lookin' forward to some peace and quiet, but now I reckon there'll be a bunch o' damn tenderfeet ruckusin' around all winter."

"Maybe not," Fargo said. "If the snow melts enough to open the pass, they plan to leave and make a run for Fort Hall."

"I'll be prayin' for good weather, then," Ed Dugan said around the stem of the pipe. He took it out of his mouth and spat eloquently on the snow-covered ground. "I was about to build a fire. Reckon I'll get back to it."

"That's what I had in mind. I'll go do that in some of the other cabins."

"As long as you don't bother me, I don't give a damn what you do."

The grouchy old-timer turned and went back into the cabin. Fargo led the Ovaro over to one of the other structures and left the stallion ground-hitched there while he went in and started a fire in the fireplace, using a few scraps of paper he found in the room as kindling. The chimney in this cabin didn't draw quite as well as in the building Ed Dugan was occupying, but it would do. When Fargo had the blaze going, he went outside and found that both Milo and Maureen had pulled into the fort and parked their wagons to one side. The other emigrant vehicles were rolling one by one through the open gates.

Milo had climbed down from his wagon, and as Fargo walked up, Maureen jumped down from hers. "I almost can't believe we're here!" she exclaimed. "I was beginning to think we'd never get back."

Fargo pointed to the cabin where he'd started a fire. "You can warm up over there."

"What about the cabin where we—" Maureen broke off the question as Milo strode up.

"It's already occupied," Fargo said quickly, to cover up any possible embarrassment on Maureen's part. "We're not the only ones here."

"What?" Milo said. "Who else is there?"

"Some old fella who's probably a trapper," Fargo explained. "His name's Dugan. He's claimed that cabin over yonder." He pointed out the cabin where Dugan was but didn't explain that it was the same building where he and Maureen had spent the previous night. Nor did he mention that Dugan had threatened to blow his head off with a shotgun. Fargo knew the old-timer hadn't been just blustering, either. But now that Dugan understood the situation, maybe he would see that there was no need for trouble.

"As long as he doesn't bother us, we won't bother him," Milo said. He turned to the others and lifted his voice as he started to give orders. "As soon as the last wagon is inside, some of you boys close those gates! We need some people to gather firewood and clean out fireplaces and chimneys. Get your teams unhitched and herd all the livestock over to the other side of the fort!"

Milo seemed to have things under control, Fargo thought. He didn't like Milo very much, and the man was inexperienced at surviving here on the frontier, but Milo was making an effort to do the right things, anyway. Given time, he would learn what to do and what not to do.

After Fargo unsaddled the stallion and led him into a makeshift pen with the rest of the horses, he went to the cabin that Dugan had claimed and rapped on the door.

"Go away!"

"It's Fargo. I just want to talk for a minute."

He thought that Dugan was going to refuse to come to the door, but then the panel was jerked open. "Speak your piece, and make it quick," Dugan snapped. There was a blaze going in the fireplace now, and the light was behind Dugan. The old-timer was still wearing the bulky coat, which Fargo could now see was made from the hide of a grizzly bear. Dugan had a fur cap pulled down over his ears, too, and lank, iron gray hair stuck out from under it.

"If you'd let me in and close the door, you could keep some of the cold air out," Fargo suggested.

"I'd rather keep you and the rest o' them pilgrims out," Dugan said. "But you're here, and I reckon you ain't goin' away." He stepped back. "Come on in."

Fargo closed the door behind him as Dugan turned toward the fireplace and held out his hands to warm them. Fargo cast a glance at the floor in front of the fireplace, remembering how lovely Maureen had looked as she lay there, nude on the buffalo robe. With a little shake of his head, Fargo put that image out of his thoughts. There was no telling when he and Maureen would have a chance to be alone again, so it would be best not to dwell on such memories, no matter how pleasant they were.

"I reckon you'd be the one who was here last night," Dugan said.

"That's right. You must have seen the tracks."

"Yep. And I could tell there's been a fire here lately in this fireplace." Dugan looked over his shoulder at Fargo, a sly expression on his narrow face. "I seen the tracks of two horses."

"One of the people from the wagon train was with me," Fargo said.

"A gal?"

"That's not any of your business." Fargo's tone was cooler now.

"Don't be so damn touchy. I didn't mean nothin'. It don't matter to me what you do, or who you do it with."

Fargo didn't care for the turn this conversation had taken. He tried to steer it back into the channels he had intended for it. "These people are short on supplies. They were robbed by the man who was pretending to guide them. He led them into a trap and had a gang waiting."

Dugan laughed. "I say them that gets fleeced was usually sheep to start with."

"They walked right into it," Fargo admitted, "but they didn't know any better. And now they're in a bad fix."

"Hell, you don't expect me to share my possibles with 'em, do you? I ain't got much, neither."

"I was just wondering how well you know these mountains."

"Been up here nigh on to thirty years," Dugan said. "I was with the expedition that built this here fort. There ain't many who know the Lost River country better'n I do. Not many who're still alive, anyway."

"Is there enough game for these people to survive?"

Dugan rubbed his bony jaw. "Quite a few moose and elk still around," he mused. "Some deer. The bears are all about to den up for the winter, so they won't be around." Dugan shrugged. "If there's one or two of the fellers who're decent hunters, I reckon they can get enough game to keep ever'body from starvin'. Those folks'll be awful tired o' moose steaks before spring rolls around, though."

"I don't care how tired they are, as long as they're still alive."

"Who appointed you their keeper, mister? What'd you say your name was, anyway?"

"Skye Fargo. And I guess I appointed myself to look after them."

"This fella who led 'em up here and then bushwhacked 'em . . . what was his name?"

"I think they called him Corrigan," Fargo said.

Dugan's thin eyebrows lifted over deep-set eyes. "Vince Corrigan?"

Fargo shook his head. "I don't know his first name."

"Got to be Vince. He's the only Corrigan I've heard of in these parts."

"You know him?" Fargo asked.

"I know of him," Dugan replied. "He's supposed to be a mean son of a bitch, about as cold-blooded as a snake. Came up here a few years ago to do some trappin' but found out it was easier to shoot good men in the back and steal their plews instead. Probably would've been hanged by now if he hadn't dropped out o' sight. Reckon he must've gone down to some o' those settlements along the Oregon Trail and gathered hisself a bunch o' outlaws just like him to set that trap for your friends."

"Vince Corrigan," Fargo repeated, fixing the name in his mind. "Maybe I'll run into him one of these days."

"If you do, you best watch your back."

"I always do," Fargo said with a tight smile.

After a moment of studying him, Dugan nodded. "Yeah, you look like you still got some o' the bark on you, Fargo. You want anything else?"

"Just your word that you won't bother any of the folks from the wagons. I know you'd rather have your privacy—"

Dugan snorted. "That's the damned truth!"

"But it wasn't their idea to get trapped up here," Fargo went on. "They'll stay out of your way if that's what you want. I'm sure, though, that if you want to be friends, you'd be more than welcome to join them while they're here."

Without hesitation, Dugan shook his head. "Nope. I'll steer clear of 'em, don't worry. I don't cotton much to people. That's one reason I come up here to the mountains a long time ago, to get away from the crowds. They leave me alone, and I'll leave them alone."

"Fair enough," Fargo said. "Who knows, maybe you'll

be lucky and the weather will improve enough for them to leave."

"That'd be just fine with me. In the meantime, you best spread the word that they should stay away from this cabin. I ain't sayin' I'll shoot anybody who comes pokin' around . . . but I ain't sayin' I won't, neither."

"All right," Fargo said. He gave Dugan a curt nod and turned to leave.

"That goes for you, too, Fargo," Dugan added. "I got nothin' against you and you seem like a good sort, but if you come sneakin' around again, there's liable to be trouble."

"I'll remember that," Fargo said, and added silently to himself, *You cantankerous old bastard.*

"He's just an old trapper who doesn't care for anybody's company except his own, like I thought," Fargo explained a short time later to Maureen and Milo.

"Can he be trusted?" Milo asked. "We can't afford to have anybody stealing any of our rations."

"I explained the situation to him. He said he'll leave you alone, and he wants to be left alone, as well. In fact, it would be a good idea if everyone knew to stay away from his cabin."

"Why?" Maureen asked.

"Well . . ." Fargo had debated whether or not to tell them about the veiled threat Dugan had made, and he had decided that they had a right to know. "He's liable to take a shot at anyone who comes poking around."

"A shot!" Milo exclaimed. "Why, that old coot! He's got no right to tell us where we can go."

"That's where you're wrong," Fargo said, his voice hardening. "That scattergun he carries gives him the right, and so does the fact that he's survived in these mountains for decades. You have to respect that. I do, anyway."

Milo glared, but after a second he nodded. "Yeah, I reckon you're right. But he'd better not hurt any of our people. I won't stand for it if he does."

Fargo wasn't sure what Milo thought he could do, but he didn't want to continue this line of discussion. "Just spread the word that the old man's not to be bothered."

"Yeah, yeah." Milo nodded. "I don't see why he should get the best cabin, though."

The three of them were in the cabin where Fargo had started the fire earlier. Cold wind whistled through gaps between the logs that would have to be chinked, and in addition to being chilly, the room was a little smoky because of the partially clogged chimney. But being in here was a lot better than being outside. The wind had picked up and the snow had started to fall heavily again.

"Dugan was here first," Fargo pointed out. "In fact, he told me he was part of the fur-trapping expedition that built this fort, nearly thirty years ago."

"That's amazing," Maureen said. "Why would anyone want to stay in this wilderness for such a long time?"

Fargo could tell from the question that Maureen had never seen the Rockies at their best, never breathed the early morning mountain air in summer, never seen an eagle wheeling through a spectacularly blue sky or walked down a green valley next to a stream that leaped and sparkled in the sun. The mountains demanded a price in hardiness and perseverance, but they repaid it tenfold with their magnificence. Maureen's inexperience wasn't her fault, though, so Fargo just smiled and said, "I reckon he's got his reasons."

"Well, I can't wait to get out of here and head for more civilized country," Milo said.

"That'll have to wait for a while. Even if the weather improves enough for you to get through the pass, the best you can hope for is to make it to Fort Hall. It'll be next summer before you see Oregon."

"I'm sure it will be worth the time it takes to get there," Maureen said.

Fargo nodded. The Pacific Northwest had its own rewards, and it was pretty country, too.

His stomach rumbled then, prompting a laugh from Maureen. "I'll see about fixing some supper," she said.

A short time later, they ate salt jowl and beans that Maureen had heated up in a pot she hung over the fire on an iron rod. They used biscuits to soak up the last of the juice from the beans when they were finished. If they had to stay here all winter, Fargo thought, by spring they would consider a meal such as this a feast. But maybe it wouldn't come to that. Maybe the wagon train would have to stay here for only a few days.

"That was mighty good," he told Maureen. "Thank you."

"You provided the meat, Skye," she said with a smile, and Fargo saw the quick frown that crossed Milo's face at her easy use of Fargo's first name. "We should be thanking you."

"No need," Fargo said. "We're all in this together now." He had been sitting cross-legged on the floor, since there was no furniture in the cabin. Now he came to his feet in one lithe motion. "It's getting late. I'd better go see about finding a place to spend the night."

Maureen looked surprised. "Why, you're going to stay here, aren't you?"

Milo's frown deepened.

"I'm not sure how proper that would be," Fargo began.

"What about Milo and me?" Maureen interrupted.

"You're related—"

"No, we ain't," Milo said. "Not really."

"There, you see," Maureen said. "You have to stay with us, Skye. You and Milo will be each other's chaperone."

Fargo could tell that Milo wasn't any happier about that idea than he was. There was nothing they could do about it as long as Maureen was being so insistent, however. And maybe she was right. Maybe it *would* be more proper this way.

"I still need to go check on my horse and the other livestock," Fargo said.

Milo grunted. "I'll go with you."

Fargo jerked his head in a curt nod. He might not be too fond of Milo, but he didn't mind having the man's help. "We'd better be sure there are guards posted, too."

"Why do we need guards? We closed the stockade gates."

"Those gates wouldn't keep out anybody who really wanted in, and besides, it wouldn't be too hard to climb the walls if there are no guards on duty. I'm not expecting trouble, but I'm not going out of my way to invite it, either."

For a second, Milo looked like he was going to argue, but it must have been an instinctive reaction on his part that was overcome by Fargo's logic. Milo nodded. "I guess you're right."

Both men put on their coats and hats. "Don't be too long," Maureen told them as she put on her own coat. "It's late, and I want to turn in as soon as I've cleaned the pot and the bowls." She followed Fargo and Milo out of the cabin and bent over just outside the door to scoop up a handful of snow. She began using it to scour out one of the bowls as the two men walked away.

As they neared the warehouse building, a man stepped out of it and raised a hand in greeting. "There's a horse in there," the man said. "What are we supposed to do with it?"

"That must be Dugan's horse," Fargo said. "I heard it earlier, when I first came up. You'll have to share the building with it tonight, I guess."

"Maybe we should just put it with the others," Milo suggested.

"I'm not going to move a man's horse without his permission, and I reckon it'll be soon enough tomorrow to ask Dugan about it."

Milo's lip curled. "You scared to go back over to his cabin tonight? Think he'll take that shotgun to you?"

"I don't see any point in risking it without a good reason," Fargo said.

"We've got four families spending the night in there," said the man who had complained about the horse. "That horse doesn't smell too good."

Fargo's lips tightened under his mustache. Some people just didn't know when they were well off. "Getting out of the snow and the wind is more important than how the place smells," he said.

The pilgrim thought it over. "Yeah, I guess so," he admitted. "What was that about the old man having a shotgun?"

"Stay away from him," Milo warned. "Tell everybody not to go around his cabin. He's crazy as a loon. He might shoot anybody who gets too close to him."

"Lord! You mean it? And we have to share the fort with him? Maybe we should just make him leave. There are enough of us to run him off."

Fargo felt a surge of anger. "Nobody's going to run anybody off," he said. "We may be here for months, so we'd damned well better learn how to get along."

"Yeah, sure," the man said, looking abashed. "I didn't mean anything by it, Mr. Fargo."

Fargo knew better. The man's suggestion had been serious. Fargo knew he was going to have to keep a close eye on things around here to keep trouble from breaking out.

"Just pass it along about leaving Dugan alone," he said. "And we'll need a couple of men from your group to stand guard later."

"Sure, Mr. Fargo."

Fargo and Milo moved on, stopping at the other cabins, all of which were occupied, to check on the people in them. Fargo warned them to take it easy with the supplies, in order to make them last as long as possible, and he and Milo worked out a rotating shift of guards. The two men who would stand the first watch were given the rifles. One man was placed at the gate and the other was positioned along the rear wall of the stockade. Because of the cold, each shift would last only an hour, and then the guards would be relieved. Fargo didn't really expect any problems in the middle of a storm like this, but it wouldn't hurt to be careful.

With those chores taken care of, Fargo and Milo headed for the corner of the fort where the animals were gathered. They were huddled against the stockade wall, getting out of the wind as much as possible. There had been a corral here at one time, and parts of the fence were still standing. The gaps had been closed by parked wagons.

Fargo rubbed the Ovaro's muzzle as the stallion stuck his head over the fence. He was satisfied that the animals would be all right unless a wolf or some other predator came along. That was another good reason to have guards posted during the night.

As Fargo turned to go back toward the cabin where they had left Maureen, Milo suddenly grasped his arm. "Did you see that?" he exclaimed.

"What?" Fargo asked. He hadn't seen anything except blowing curtains of snow that swept across the open ground inside the stockade.

"Over there by the warehouse," Milo said, pointing. "I thought I saw something moving around."

Fargo squinted but didn't see anything unusual. He could make out the dark bulk of the building through the snow, but nothing was moving.

"Must have been somebody stepping out to relieve themselves, or getting something out of a wagon."

Milo shook his head. "I know all those folks. Whoever I saw was too big to have been one of them."

Fargo frowned. He thought Milo's eyes were playing tricks on him, but it was just possible that something had gotten into the stockade. Or maybe one of the horses had gotten out of the makeshift pen and was wandering around over there.

"It looked like a bear," Milo said.

Fargo stiffened, remembering the "monster" Maureen had claimed was in the cabin that morning. She had said that it looked like a bear. But Fargo had determined that nothing like that could have been in the cabin. The lack of tracks in the snow had proven that. Was Milo seeing things now?

"Maybe we should go take a look," Fargo said slowly. He wanted to get to the bottom of this. He didn't like mysteries.

He and Milo walked through the snow toward the

warehouse. "It was right there at the corner," Milo said, pointing. "I just caught a glimpse of it, and then it was gone, like it ducked back around the building."

Fargo rested his hand on the butt of his Colt. He didn't believe they were going to find anything; he still thought it had been Milo's imagination, just as it had been a dream with Maureen that morning. But on the off chance that something unfriendly really was back there . . .

As they reached the corner of the building, the possibility crossed Fargo's mind that maybe Milo was trying to lure him back there so that he could attack him. If Milo really was jealous of Maureen, he might be angry enough with Fargo to start a fight, especially if he had any inkling of what had gone on between them the night before. But Fargo discarded that idea after a moment. If all Milo wanted was to take a punch at him, he could have done that long before now. There was no reason to lure Fargo behind the warehouse with some crazy story.

Besides, Milo sounded sincere—and a little frightened. "It was right here," he said as they paused at the corner. "I know I saw it."

Fargo looked down at the ground. The wind was whipping around the building and blowing the snow, blotting out any tracks almost as soon as they were made. Fargo glanced over his shoulder. He could barely see the prints he and Milo had made trudging over here.

"Let's take a look," Fargo said, his fingers tightening on the walnut grips of the heavy revolver.

He stepped around the corner. Milo hesitated for a heartbeat, then came with him. It was hard to see anything back there. Fargo wished for a torch, but the wind and the snow would have put it out almost immediately. He reached out with his left hand and rested his fingers against the logs that formed the rear wall of the warehouse, trailing them along the wall as he walked so that he wouldn't veer to the side. He turned his head and raised his voice to call over the wind to Milo, "See anything?"

Milo's only reply was a sudden, startled, choked-off cry.

Fargo whirled around and yelled, "Milo!" The man had been right there, and now, without any warning, he was gone, vanished into the storm.

But something had replaced him, something huge and dark, and it moved like a freight train as it barreled down on Fargo. The Trailsman pulled his gun, but before he could bring it up, it was swatted out of his hand.

Then, looming over him, the thing fell on him like a mountain, smashing him down into blackness.

6

Fargo was never sure if he completely lost consciousness at that moment. If he did, it was only for a span of a few heartbeats. Then he became aware of the crushing weight on top of him and the awful stench that filled his nostrils. His right arm was pinned to his body by the mass of whatever had attacked him, but his left arm was free enough for him to strike upward with a closed fist. The surface he hit was covered with fur. The blow seemed to have no effect whatsoever.

A grizzly, Fargo thought wildly. One of the huge, vicious creatures must have gotten inside the stockade. Old Ephraim, the fur trappers of an earlier era had nicknamed the beast. Fargo had no idea why. But he knew how dangerous grizzlies were. If one of them was attacking him now, he had only seconds to live. The bear's claws and teeth would shred his flesh and rip his guts out.

The thing didn't claw at him, though. Instead it seemed to be trying to crush him with its sheer weight. Its hot, foul breath filled Fargo's nostrils as the creature grunted and slobbered. Fargo hit it again, and this time the weight on top of him seemed to shift.

Fargo didn't waste any time seizing what might be the only opportunity he would have. His back arched off the snow-covered ground, and he threw all his strength into a roll. The creature came off of him, toppling to the side. Fargo's right arm was free now, but numb and useless. He reached down with his left hand instead and jerked the Arkansas toothpick from its sheath in his boot. As the thing came at him again, Fargo lashed out with the toothpick. The blade encountered resistance, then sliced through whatever was balking it. Fargo felt the vibration in his arm as the knife scraped along something hard: a rib, maybe.

The creature let out a howl of pain. Fargo snatched the knife back and struck again. This time he missed, hitting only empty air because the thing had jerked aside in reaction to being stabbed. Fargo swung his arm in a backhanded slash and felt the blade drag across something.

What felt like the trunk of a small tree smashed into the side of Fargo's head and sent him sprawling face-down in the snow. His mouth and nose filled with the cold, powdery stuff. He sputtered and coughed as he lifted his head, fighting for breath.

He expected the creature to jump him again. He had lost his grip on the toothpick when he fell, so he reached across his body for the Colt. It was gone, too. The fingers of Fargo's left hand found an empty holster. He would have to face the next attack armed with only his bare hands, and his right arm still didn't want to work correctly. He knew he should have yelled for help, but he couldn't get his breath. The weight of the thing landing on top of him had knocked all the air out of his lungs, and he hadn't recovered enough to be able to shout.

But instead of some ravening beast coming out of the storm at him, all that hit Fargo was the snow that was still falling. He pushed himself onto his hands and knees and stood up shakily. His eyes narrowed as he peered into the swirling clouds of snow. He didn't see anything else. Whatever the creature had been, it seemed to be gone.

Fargo dragged in several deep breaths. His head was ringing from the blow that had laid him out in the snow, and his heart was pounding heavily in his chest. Gradually, those reactions began to subside. His jumbled thoughts became clearer. He turned and called, "Milo! Milo, are you there?"

A faint groan came in answer to Fargo's shouts. Fargo

listened intently as the sound came again and then stumbled toward it. A moment later he almost tripped over a bulky body stretched out in the snow.

Fargo went to a knee beside the man and reached out to touch him. He was lying facedown, so Fargo grasped his shoulders and rolled him over. Fargo felt a bushy beard growing on the man's chin and knew that he had found Milo. A quick check of his body found no wounds, but there was a good-sized lump on Milo's head where he had been hit, or been rammed into something. Fargo put a hand behind Milo's neck and lifted his head, then started patting his cheek with the other hand. "Milo! Milo, wake up."

Milo groaned again and started to stir. Suddenly, he began to flail around, and Fargo had to draw back to avoid the wild blows.

"Milo, take it easy!" Fargo said, his tone urgent enough to get through to the man. "It's me, Fargo. Stop!"

Milo stopped swinging his arms. He clutched at Fargo instead. "F-Fargo?" he whispered.

"That's right. What happened to you?"

"Ohhhh," Milo moaned. "Help me sit up."

Fargo did so, and Milo put his hands to his head. "Feels like somebody dropped a mountain on me."

Fargo grunted. "I know the feeling. Whatever it was jumped me, too."

Milo gripped Fargo's arm. "Then there really was something?"

"That's right."

"I knew it felt like something grabbed me, but I . . . I wasn't sure. I remember I started to yell . . . then something had me by the throat. It . . . it picked me up like that and threw me . . . I must've hit my head when I landed."

"You've got a goose egg on your skull, all right," Fargo confirmed. "And after that thing flung you out of the way, it came after me."

"How come you're not dead?" Milo asked. "It was a bear, wasn't it?"

Fargo considered the question for a moment. "I thought so at first. Now . . . I'm not so sure. It didn't seem to have any claws. And when I got my knife out and stuck it a couple of times, it ran off. A grizzly wouldn't have done that."

"You're sure?"

"Sure enough," Fargo said. "Men have killed grizzlies with a knife before, but not without getting torn up awful bad themselves."

"Maybe you were just lucky."

Fargo considered his pounding head and the aches that were already starting all over his body. "Yeah," he said. "Lucky."

Actually, he *was* lucky to be alive, and he knew it. The creature could have overpowered him and choked the life out of him. If he had lost consciousness and stayed out, that was what would have happened. Fargo was sure of it. He had been able to feel the rage radiating off the creature in waves. It had wanted to kill him.

Fargo got a hand under one of Milo's arms. "Let's get you back to the cabin."

Milo struggled to his feet with Fargo's help and asked, "How come the guards didn't come to see what all the commotion was about?"

"They must not have heard all the yelling over the wind. It's a pretty good way to the gate."

"Yeah, but the fella posted back here at the wall should have been able to hear us."

Fargo knew Milo was right. "Let's go take a look," he suggested.

He was acutely aware that he no longer had his revolver or his knife; it would be almost impossible to find them in the snow until daylight came again. Milo was unarmed as well. But if they could find the guard, he would have one of the rifles.

A grim feeling began to grow inside Fargo as he and Milo found the rear wall of the stockade and began making their way along it. The snow wasn't falling quite as heavily now, but the night was still so dark that it was impossible to see more than a foot or two. Fargo didn't spot the guard's body until he tripped over it.

"Here," he said as he knelt next to the fallen form. His hands explored the man's torso and moved up to his shoulders.

"Wait a minute," Milo said. "My foot just hit something over here. Let me see what it is . . . *Yahhhh!*" He jumped back so fast he lost his balance and sat down hard in the snow. "It's a *head!*"

Fargo swallowed the feeling of nausea that welled up. He wasn't surprised by Milo's horrified exclamation. He had already discovered that the body by which he was kneeling lacked a head on its shoulders.

"Something twisted it right off," Fargo said. "The same thing that jumped us, I reckon."

"You . . . you mean it could have . . . we could have lost our . . ." Milo fell silent, and a second later Fargo heard him retching.

Fargo felt around in the snow near the body, and this time he was lucky. His fingers found a long, hard shape and pulled a Henry rifle out of the snow by the barrel. He brushed off the rifle and checked it over, working the lever to jack a cartridge into the chamber. His expert touch told him the weapon was in good working order.

He got to his feet. "We'd better get back to the cabin."

"Yeah." Milo's voice was choked with fear. "Maureen's there by herself!"

Fargo had thought of the same thing already. "Let's go."

Clutching the rifle tightly, Fargo led the way. He and Milo were silent now. In the face of the violence and horror they had encountered tonight, there was really nothing to say. It would take time for their minds to grasp what had happened. And Fargo was sure that Milo was just as worried about Maureen as he was.

She gasped as the two men burst into the cabin a few minutes later. She was sitting on the floor in front of the fire with her knees drawn up and her arms around them.

Looking back over her shoulder at Fargo and Milo, she asked, "What's wrong? You two look like you've seen a ghost!"

"No, not a ghost," Fargo said.

"But a dead man, sure enough," Milo added.

Maureen got to her feet hurriedly. "Oh, no! One of our people?"

Milo nodded. "The Ellison boy. He was on guard at the back wall of the stockade. Something jumped Fargo and me, but before that it must have attacked Steve, probably while we were checking on the animals."

Fargo had reached the same conclusion. Whatever the creature had been, it had killed the guard, then attacked him and Milo when they came looking for it behind the warehouse.

Maureen put a hand to her mouth in horror. "That's awful," she whispered. "That poor young man. I . . . I can't believe it."

"Believe it," Fargo said. "Milo and I both had a run-in with it."

Understanding dawned in Maureen's eyes as she looked at Fargo. "Skye," she said in a hushed voice, "it . . . it must have been the same thing I saw this morning."

"What?" Milo said. He frowned. "What are you talking about, Maureen?"

"I saw something here at the fort this morning before Skye and I left," she explained. "It was some sort of . . . some sort of monster. I had convinced myself it wasn't real, but now . . ."

"I'm sorry, Maureen," Fargo said. "I still don't understand it, but I reckon you were right about what you saw. The thing that attacked us was about as big as a bear, and it had fur like one. But I'm convinced it wasn't a grizzly."

"Did you see its face?"

Fargo shook his head. "Out there in the storm and the dark, it was hard to see anything. All I know for sure is that it was big and strong and smelled terrible."

"That's it," Maureen declared with a nod. "That's what I saw—and smelled." A shudder went through her. "I almost think it was better when I believed I had imagined it."

Fargo knew what she meant. It was pretty disquieting to think that something huge and bloodthirsty was roaming around the fort, with the ability to vanish seemingly at will without leaving any tracks.

"We need a lantern so we can take a look around," Milo said. "I want to kill that thing."

Fargo couldn't argue with that sentiment, but he didn't like the idea of leaving Maureen alone again. "I want everyone to gather in the warehouse," he said. "That way they can look out for each other while we're searching for the creature."

"That's a good idea. Do we pull in the guard from the gate?"

Fargo nodded. "Yes. I want a rifle in the warehouse so the group will have some protection." He tightened his grip on the Henry. "Maureen, put your coat on, and let's go."

Moments later they left the cabin and went from building to building inside the fort, telling the other pilgrims to get whatever they needed for the night and congregate in the warehouse. Fargo herded the group along as it grew, ignoring the puzzled questions for the moment. Maureen could explain everything to them once they were all safely inside the big log building.

Milo pointed at the cabin where Ed Dugan was staying. "What about the old coot?"

Fargo thought it over, and said, "Get everyone else inside the warehouse. I'll go tell Dugan what happened."

He walked to the cabin and banged his fist against the door, then stepped aside in case Dugan jerked it open and fired the shotgun. Instead, the old man called irritably, "Who the hell's out there?"

"It's Fargo. Open up, Dugan. I need to talk to you."

"Go to hell! I told you to leave me alone!"

"A man's been killed!" Fargo shouted back.

For a moment, Dugan made no reply. Then the door swung back and the old-timer stepped into the opening. "Killed, you say?"

"That's right," Fargo told him. "We had a man on guard along the rear wall of the stockade. Something pulled his head right off his shoulders."

Dugan let out a harsh laugh that made anger rise inside Fargo. "Sounds like the unlucky son of a bitch ran into the Lost River Lurker."

"What are you talking about?" Fargo demanded.

"You never heard of the Lost River Lurker?" Dugan laughed again. "Hell, son, the gents who've trapped this valley have known about it for years. The Lurker's torn more than one man to pieces when he was unlucky enough to stumble onto it."

"What *is* it?"

Dugan shook his head. "I don't rightly know. Don't reckon anybody does. But accordin' to the story, the Lurker is half man, half bear, with maybe a little bit of some other critters thrown in. And he's damned unfriendly, too. If he can get his paws on you, he'll kill you, sure as hell."

"He had his paws on me tonight," Fargo said, "and all he got for his trouble was my Arkansas toothpick stuck in him."

Dugan stiffened. "You stabbed the Lurker?"

"That's right."

"Why, you crazy bastard." Dugan's voice was hollow with fear. "The Lurker don't usually stay around one place for long. But if you hurt him, he won't never leave for good until he's settled the score."

Fargo's eyes narrowed with suspicion. "You sound like you know an awful lot about this thing, whatever it really is."

"I told you, I been around these mountains for a long time!" the old trapper snapped. "Long enough to see the bodies o' the men the Lurker killed. I seen him myself a few times . . . from a good ways off, mind you . . . and I don't want to see him again." Dugan shook his head. "You've played hob, Fargo. You've invited hell down on all of us."

"What was I supposed to do?" Fargo shot back. "Lie there and let the thing kill me?"

"The rest of us might've been better off." Dugan sighed and went on, "But I reckon the damage is already done, and there ain't no way to undo it. You better get all your people together in one place where you can keep an eye on 'em."

"We've already done that. They're in the warehouse building."

"Good idea. They got any guns?"

"Just a Henry rifle."

Dugan rubbed his jaw. "Likely that ain't goin' to be enough if the Lurker comes callin'. He's been shot no tellin' how many times over the years, and he just keeps on a-comin'. To tell you the truth, it might take a cannon to bring him down. You ain't got a cannon, have you?"

"Of course not," Fargo said. "The closest one is probably at Fort Hall."

"Well, that won't do you any good. You'll just have to make do with what you got." Dugan jerked his head toward the warehouse. "Better go on over there and keep an eye on those greenhorns. Don't let any of 'em out before mornin' if you want 'em to stay alive."

"What about you?" Fargo asked.

Dugan snorted. "You think I want to sit around some drafty old warehouse with a bunch of scared, gabblin' fools? I'll stay right here by my ownself, thank you very much."

"You're not afraid of this Lost River Lurker?"

"I know how to steer clear o' trouble. Been doin' it for a damned long time. I'll be fine."

Fargo didn't want to leave Dugan on his own, but he didn't want to stand around arguing the matter, either. Apparently, Dugan knew more about the danger represented by the creature than any of the rest of them did, so if the old-timer wanted to stay here in the cabin, that was his decision to make.

"You don't have any guns you can spare us, do you?"

"Nope, I sure don't. Even if I did, I wouldn't give 'em to you. Last thing I want is a bunch o' scared, trigger-happy greenhorns traipsin' around any place I'm stayin'."

With that, Dugan stepped back and closed the door firmly in Fargo's face.

Fargo resisted the impulse to kick the door open and give Dugan a piece of his mind. It wouldn't do any good, he realized. The old trapper was too set in his belligerent ways for anything to change his thinking.

He went back to the warehouse and called out his own name before going inside so that no one would take a shot at him. He found the entire company of emigrants huddled together around the fire, fear on their faces. Milo had the other rifle. He came toward Fargo and asked, "Where's the old man?"

"He won't come over here," Fargo said. "Claims he'd rather stay right where he is."

"Damned old fool," Milo muttered. "Did he have any idea what that thing was?"

Fargo inclined his head toward the door. He didn't want to spread a panic by repeating Dugan's story about the Lost River Lurker where the others could hear. For one thing, Fargo didn't believe in creatures that were half man, half animal. On the other hand, he had heard plenty of stories in his travels about such beasts as the Wendigo. Every Indian tribe had their own tales and legends about monsters. Down in Texas one time, he had even heard about one that was supposed to be half man and half goat. And whether he wanted to believe in creatures like that or not, Fargo had to admit that he had no explanation for what he and Milo had encountered tonight.

Milo followed him to the doorway. "Dugan spun some yarn about a varmint called the Lost River Lurker," Fargo told him. "He says it's half man and half bear, and supposedly it's been killing trappers in this valley for years."

"Son of a bitch," Milo breathed. "You think it's true?"

"I don't know what to think," Fargo admitted. "But

I'm going to take a look around out there. You stay in here with that rifle and be ready for trouble."

Milo frowned. "You shouldn't be wandering around out there by yourself, Fargo. That thing nearly killed both of us."

"It won't sneak up on me this time," Fargo said. "And I'll have a light with me, too."

"How are you going to keep a lantern burning in this weather?"

"The wind's died down a little. I don't think it'll blow out the flame if I'm careful."

"You'd better be damned careful, Fargo," Milo said. "I don't much like admitting this, but I reckon we'd be in a lot worse shape if you hadn't come along when you did. I'm not sure I could get us out of this mess if anything happened to you."

Fargo grinned. "You'd do all right," he said, liking Milo better now since the terrifying events of the evening had taken his arrogance down a notch. "I'll get the lantern out of Maureen's wagon."

"That'd be best, I reckon, since you know where it is," Milo agreed.

Fargo clapped his free hand on Milo's shoulder and turned to the door. As he slipped out, he heard Maureen say, "Milo, where's Skye going?"

He didn't hear the answer because he had pulled the door shut behind him by then. The wind wasn't as strong as it had been earlier, but it still tugged at his hat and blew snow around him. Fargo tramped toward Maureen's wagon. When he reached it, he climbed inside and snapped a lucifer to life with the thumbnail of his free hand. The sulfur match's glare helped him find the lantern, and he was able to light the wick before the match burned out. The yellow glow that filled the back of the wagon was comforting.

Fargo couldn't stay there, though. He stepped back out, holding the lantern in his left hand and keeping it close to his body in an effort to shield it from the wind. The flame wavered but didn't go out. Fargo circled the warehouse. The rifle was in his right hand, with a shell resting in the chamber and Fargo's finger just outside the trigger guard.

He paused at the spot where he and Milo had run into the creature. The marks of the struggle were still visible in the snow, though the wind and the continuing snowfall were beginning to blur them. Fargo saw dark spots against the white and bent closer for a better look. The spots were small spatters of blood, just as he had thought. Whatever the Lost River Lurker might be—if there was such a thing—it bled when cold steel cut it. That was a little reassuring, Fargo thought. Anything that bled could be killed.

He stood up and spent a few moments looking around for his Colt and the Arkansas toothpick. Not finding them, he moved on to the place he and Milo had found the dead guard's body. Fargo forced himself to look at the bloody destruction that had been wreaked. Several yards separated the body from the head. Milo had picked it up to see what it was, then tossed it aside in shock and horror. Fargo held the lantern so that its light shone on the face of the unfortunate young man. He wore an expression of surprise, but his face showed little pain. The creature had wrenched his head off so fast that he probably hadn't even known what was happening. Fargo hoped fervently that was the case.

His eyes searched the snow for tracks. He found some leading along the stockade wall and followed them. When they stopped, Fargo looked up at the wall. This was where the creature had climbed in, he decided. Or climbed out, maybe. The tracks were too indistinct for him to be able to tell if they were coming or going.

Fargo grimaced. He hoped that the Lurker was gone, but there was no proof of that. It could still be in the fort somewhere. A moment passed before he realized that he had thought of the creature by the name Dugan had used. *Well, why not,* he asked himself. That was as good a name as any.

Suddenly, Fargo lifted his head. He thought he'd heard a shout. The sound had been faint, most of it carried off by the wind, and he couldn't even be sure that it had been made by a human voice. It could have been a limb breaking under the weight of the snow.

But then he heard it again, and this time he was sure it was a voice calling. He ran through the snow toward the warehouse, thinking that maybe there was trouble inside.

Before he could get there, however, he heard more voices. Several men were calling back and forth through the storm, and the shouts were coming from outside the stockade. Fargo swung toward the gate. As he reached Maureen's wagon, he blew out the lantern and set it on the seat. His natural caution made him kneel beside one of the wagon's rear wheels. He held the rifle in both hands now, ready to bring it to his shoulder. Whoever was approaching the fort might well be friendly, but Fargo wasn't going to assume that without proof. The most likely explanation, though, was that more trappers like Ed Dugan were coming to spend the winter here.

This old stockade was a mighty busy place tonight, Fargo thought with a brief, humorless smile.

He watched as the gates swung open and several men led horses into the fort. There were close to a dozen of them, Fargo estimated. They were clad in heavy coats, but they were stumbling along as if they had been trudging through the storm for a long time and were half-frozen and exhausted. Fargo didn't move as he watched them come on a few steps.

Then the man in the lead stopped short and let out a startled exclamation as he looked around and saw the parked wagons and the livestock. "Son of a bitch! It's that same damned bunch of pilgrims!"

That told Fargo all he needed to know, and what he had already guessed was confirmed a second later when one of the men asked, "What do we do now, Vince?"

Fargo knew he was looking at the gang of outlaws that had looted the wagon train, along with their leader, Vince Corrigan. Which just went to prove the old saying—

Things were never so bad that they couldn't get worse.

7

Fargo stood absolutely still for a moment while he thought feverishly. Where he was, the wagon wheel concealed him to a certain extent, and given the darkness of the night, he was confident the outlaws hadn't spotted him when they entered the fort. But Corrigan and his men had seen the wagons and the livestock. It would have been almost impossible to miss them. In a matter of minutes, those hard cases and killers would start investigating the buildings inside the stockade, and they would find the group of emigrants in the old warehouse with only one rifle to protect them.

Sometimes one rifle was enough, though, if a man used it right, Fargo thought grimly. He couldn't delay any longer. He had to run a bluff and let everything ride on the bet.

He lined the barrel of the Henry on the ground a few feet in front of Corrigan and pulled the trigger. The rifle cracked, and the bullet sent snow flying in the air as it plowed into the ground. "Hold it!" Fargo shouted, his powerful voice cutting through the sound of the wind. "Nobody move! You're covered!"

Corrigan had jumped back at the sound of the shot and started to draw his pistol. He froze that way, in an awkward crouch. "What the hell!"

"You boys drop your guns and move away from them," Fargo ordered. "There's a whole troop of cavalry with rifles lined up on you right now."

"Damn, Vince!" one of the outlaws said. "It's the army! Those pilgrims must've sicced the army on us!"

"Shut up," Corrigan snapped. "I don't see no troopers."

"But they can see you," Fargo said. "Drop your guns now, or we'll drop you!"

Tension had every nerve in his body stretched tight. If his bluff worked, maybe he could disarm the outlaws before they realized he was only one man. Then he could herd them into one of the unused buildings and figure out some way to lock them inside. But that would work only if he could get them moving before they stopped to think too much.

"I don't see no cavalry horses," Corrigan said. "Looks to me like there's nobody here but those stupid bastards from that wagon train."

That was exactly what Fargo didn't want the outlaw leader thinking. He was about to put a slug in Corrigan's shoulder to impress the others that they'd better do as they were told, when the sound of a woman's voice came floating through the cold night air.

"Skye! Skye, where are you?"

Fargo bit back a curse. It was Maureen. What the hell was she doing out here?

Hard on the heels of her call, Milo shouted, "Damn it, Maureen, get back in here—"

"Scatter!" Corrigan yelled. He jerked his gun from its holster and triggered two shots toward Fargo as the rest of the outlaw band spread out and scurried for cover. The blasts were still echoing in the frigid air as Corrigan ducked back among the milling horses.

Maureen must have heard the shot he'd fired in front of Corrigan and gotten scared that something had happened to him, Fargo thought as he swung the barrel of the Henry and snapped off a shot at one of the outlaws who was still visible, though running for cover. The man yelped and tumbled off his feet. Fargo ducked back farther behind the wagon as several of Corrigan's men opened fire on him. Bullets thudded into the prairie schooner's body and ripped through its canvas cover.

Fargo hoped that Maureen had the sense to get back inside the warehouse. He didn't have time to worry about her right now. Moving in a crouch, he went to the other end of the wagon and leaned against it, thrusting the barrel of the Henry around it and searching for a fresh target. He felt the vibrations against his shoulder as bullets continued to strike the wagon.

"There's no cavalry!" Corrigan yelled. "It's just one man. Rush the son of a bitch!"

Fargo started to fall back toward the far side of the stockade. He wanted to lead the outlaws away from the warehouse where the emigrants were holed up. He suspected that he was just prolonging the inevitable, but the Trailsman wasn't the sort to give up without a fight. He broke into a run, firing twice from the hip as he sprinted through the snow. Slugs sizzled around his head as the outlaws gave chase.

Where was the Lost River Lurker when a fella really needed him? Fargo would have liked to drop that monster, whatever it really was, right down in the middle of Corrigan and his gang.

His path took him past the cabin occupied by Ed Dugan. The old mountain man took him by surprise, flinging the door open and calling, "Fargo! Over here!"

As Fargo veered toward the cabin, Dugan lifted an old Sharps carbine and pointed it at him. A heart-stopping instant later, Fargo realized that Dugan wasn't aiming *at* him, but rather *past* him. The heavy caliber buffalo gun roared, spewing flame and sparks from its muzzle as Dugan fired. Some bullets made a sound like a whining mosquito when they passed close to a man's head; the slug thrown by the Sharps gave off a roar like a bull fiddle. Fargo heard two distinct cries behind him and figured Dugan had dropped a pair of outlaws with a single bullet. He had carried a Sharps for a while and knew that one of its bullets could blow a fist-sized hole through a man and still pack plenty of punch to knock down another.

Fargo dived past Dugan into the cabin. Dugan backed

into the building after him, triggering a six-gun as he did so. The old trapper kicked the door closed.

"I used my bowie to carve out some o' the chinks between logs so we'd have places to shoot at those rascals," Dugan told Fargo. "I heard the yellin', figured it was Corrigan, and knew that hell was likely to pop!"

Fargo thrust the barrel of the Henry through one of the little apertures that Dugan had made in the wall. He fired three times as fast as he could work the rifle's lever, spraying the bullets across the open area in the middle of the stockade. That might cause Corrigan's men to go to ground for a short time. Dugan opened the door a crack, stuck out the twin barrels of his shotgun, and touched off both of them. The weapon's roar was deafening in the close confines of the cabin. Fargo barely heard Dugan's cackling laughter and the old man's cry of "That'll make 'em hop!"

Fargo withdrew the rifle from the makeshift firing port and reached in his pocket for fresh shells. The Henry still held several shots, but Fargo wanted it fully loaded before Corrigan's gang charged the cabin.

Because he figured that was what was coming. Within minutes, Corrigan's men would rush the cabin.

Unless they did something smarter, Fargo realized, like go after the other people here in the fort. That was what he really had to be afraid of.

"That is Corrigan out there, ain't it?" Dugan asked.

"Yeah," Fargo said. "I heard a couple of his men call him Vince."

"I been wonderin' when they'd show up."

Fargo looked over his shoulder at the old man. "What do you mean?"

"You said Corrigan and his bunch robbed that wagon train. He cut it too close, though. This storm moved in 'fore they had a chance to get clear of the mountains. Likely they planned to hit the Salmon River and then cut over toward Fort Boise, but they were too late."

Fargo nodded. The firing had stopped outside for the moment. He didn't know if that was a good sign or a bad one. Likely bad, he decided.

"So they turned around and came looking for shelter," he said, continuing Dugan's line of thought. "This old fort was the closest place they could get out of the storm."

"Yep, that's the way it looks to me. So now you and your friends got your hands full o' even more trouble than you had before."

"You, too," Fargo pointed out with a quick grin. "You took cards in this hand when you opened up on Corrigan's bunch."

"Yeah, and it was a damn fool play, too," Dugan grumbled. "I should'a just hunkered down and hoped they wouldn't find me. Either that or slipped out the back way."

Fargo was about to ask what he meant by that when a shout sounded outside. "Hey, in the cabin! You sons o' bitches hear me?"

Fargo and Dugan exchanged a glance, then Fargo called back, "Yeah, we hear you!" The outlaws knew they were in here. Being stubborn and refusing to answer wouldn't accomplish a thing.

"Then you better listen close!" The grating voice belonged to Corrigan, Fargo thought. He had heard it enough already to be sure of that.

Suddenly, someone cried out in pain. Fargo's hands tightened on the rifle. The scream sounded like it came from a woman, and he had a bad feeling that he knew who she was.

"Let her go, or I swear I'll kill you, Corrigan!" Fargo shouted

That threat drew a laugh from the outlaw leader, which was no more or less than Fargo expected. "You ain't in any position to be bossin' us around, mister! I'm not sure how many of you are in there, but you'd better open that door, throw out all your guns, and come out with your hands up—or this bitch dies!"

"I reckon he'll do it," Dugan said in a low voice. "From what I've heard o' Corrigan, he'd slit that gal's throat and never blink an eye."

"What will he do if we surrender, like he wants?" Fargo asked.

Dugan's narrow shoulders rose and fell in a shrug. "Kill us all, more'n likely. But maybe it'll take him a while to get around to it."

Before Fargo could say anything else, a fresh round of gunfire broke out. Fargo crouched and waited for the bullets to smack into the cabin walls, but that didn't happen. This time, the shots appeared to be directed somewhere else. The furious firing died away after a minute, to be replaced by an even more ominous silence.

Corrigan's arrogant voice came again. "We got us a real live hero out here. Must be a friend of yours. He tried to sneak up on us, but all he got for his trouble was a bullet!"

A new voice bellowed, "Do what he says, Fargo! He'll . . . uh . . . he'll kill Maureen if you don't."

Fargo's jaw tightened. That was Milo Haydon. Corrigan's men must have grabbed Maureen when she came out of the warehouse to look for Fargo, and Milo had tried to rescue her only to be captured as well. The grunt of pain in the middle of Milo's plea for Fargo and Dugan to surrender probably meant that he had been wounded in the exchange of shots. He would have the other rifle with him, so now the people hiding in the warehouse truly were defenseless except for their bare hands and maybe a few tools from the wagons that could be used as clubs. They wouldn't be able to hold off Corrigan's gang.

"I sure don't like giving up," Fargo said, "but if we stay here, they'll root us out and kill us sooner or later."

"We'd send some o' them to hell first," Dugan pointed out.

"Yes, but as long as we're alive, we have a chance to turn the tables on Corrigan."

"Surrenderin' to the likes o' that bunch is a mighty bitter pill." Dugan sighed. "But you're right, Fargo. A slim chance is better than none, and none is what we got in the long run if we stay here."

They looked at each other for a moment, then each

man nodded in agreement. No more needed to be said. Fargo put his mouth close to one of the holes in the wall and shouted, "Hold your fire! We're coming out!"

"Skye, *no!*" That was Maureen. Her cry was stifled quickly. Fargo wondered if one of the outlaws had struck her.

He was going to enjoy bringing Corrigan and the rest of the bandits to justice, Fargo thought. And failing that, he wouldn't mind too much if he had to kill them.

He went to the door and used his foot to push it open. Holding the rifle in one hand, he thrust his arm out and tossed the weapon onto the snowy ground. "That's the only gun I've got!" he called.

"What about the other gent in there?" Corrigan demanded. "I know he's got at least a Sharps and a scattergun. Let's see 'em!"

"I'm gonna enjoy carvin' that hairpin a new gullet," Dugan muttered as he came to the door and threw his carbine and shotgun out where the gang could see them. He followed the long gun with his old cap and ball revolver.

"Better get rid of any knives or tomahawks or anything like that!" Corrigan warned. "If we find any blades on you, it'll go hard for you!"

As if Corrigan didn't plan to kill them already, Fargo thought. "I lost my Arkansas toothpick and my Colt in the snow earlier tonight!" he called.

"Here's my bowie, you polecats!" Dugan said as he threw out the long, heavy knife. He added under his breath, "Lord, I hate givin' it up."

"Is that all the weapons?" Fargo asked quietly.

Dugan cast a quick look around, as if afraid that someone was going to overhear what he was about to say. "Naw, there's an old pepperbox hidden over there behind a loose rock in the fireplace. If you need it and can get your hands on it later, count down five rocks from the upper left corner and three over. That's the loose one."

Fargo nodded, storing that bit of information in his brain. It might turn out to be vital—or it might mean nothing at all. He would just have to wait and see how the hand played out.

"If that's all, come on out with your paws elevated!" Corrigan ordered. "Make it fast now, before I lose my patience!"

With his jaw clenched tight in frustration, Fargo stepped out through the open door. He raised his hands to shoulder level and kept them there as he walked forward. Behind him, Dugan followed suit.

The outlaws had been using the parked wagons for cover. They came out of concealment now, and each man had a gun lined on Fargo and Dugan. Corrigan was the last one to emerge. He dragged a struggling figure with him. "Let go of me!" Maureen said to him.

"Glad to oblige, bitch," Corrigan said as he shoved Maureen roughly ahead of him. She cried out as she stumbled, lost her balance, and fell headlong into the snow. Corrigan's booted foot came down hard in the middle of her back. At the same time, he drew his revolver, pointed the barrel at the back of her head, and pulled back the hammer.

The snowfall had just about stopped, and Fargo could see well enough to make out what Corrigan was doing. Thinking that the outlaw was about to kill Maureen, he tensed his muscles, getting ready to make a leap at Corrigan in a last-ditch attempt to stop him. But then Corrigan said to Fargo and Dugan, "Is there anybody else in that cabin? Better not lie to me, there'll be chunks of her brains splattered all over that nice white snow."

Maureen whimpered softly from terror and pain.

With an effort, Fargo controlled his raging emotions. He had to stay cool now if they were going to have any chance to survive. "It's empty," he said to Corrigan. "Take a look for yourself if you don't believe me."

Corrigan made a flicking motion with his free hand. A couple of the bandits ran forward brandishing rifles and ducked into the cabin that Fargo and Dugan had just vacated. A few seconds later, they reappeared and one of them said, "He's tellin' the truth, Vince. There's nobody else in there. No guns or knives, either."

"Good," Corrigan said. He grinned at Fargo and Dugan. "You two are finally showin' some sense."

"Gonna shoot us now?" Dugan demanded harshly.

Corrigan frowned a little as he studied the old trapper. "Who are you?" he asked. "Seems I ought to know you."

Dugan gave a sniff of contempt. "You maybe seen me around, back when you was pretendin' to be an honest trapper. Name's Dugan. Ed Dugan."

"Sorry to disappoint you, old man, but I don't remember you." Corrigan looked at Fargo. "How about you? What do they call you?"

Fargo gestured at Maureen, who had fallen silent but was still pinned to the ground by Corrigan's heavy boot. "Let the lady up first."

Corrigan stepped back, but he kept the gun pointed at Maureen's head. "Tell me your name, and you can come get her."

"Fargo."

"I thought that's what that other pilgrim called you. Where'd you and this old terrapin come from, Fargo? The two of you weren't with that wagon train when I was leadin' it up here."

"Leading it into a trap, you mean?" Fargo snapped. He stepped forward, ignoring Corrigan's gun, and knelt beside Maureen. He slipped his arms around her and helped her to her feet. She clutched at him, buried her face against his chest, and sobbed.

"Skye, th-they . . . they shot Milo!"

One of the other outlaws standing around let out a whistle. "Vince, she called him Skye. That means he's Skye Fargo, the one they call the Trailsman!"

Corrigan shook his head. "That don't mean nothin' to me. Never heard of him, either." To Fargo, he said, "You didn't answer my question, Mr. Trailsman." His tone was full of scorn and sarcasm.

Fargo held Maureen and looked over her shoulder at Corrigan. "I came across the wagon train after you robbed it," he said. "We came up the valley when the storm blocked the pass. Figured we could wait for the snow to melt here at this old fort, or even spend the winter here if we had to. Dugan thought the same thing."

"Trapper, eh?" Corrigan said as he looked at Dugan. "Yeah, I probably saw you at some of the tradin' posts, or at a rendezvous."

Dugan snorted. "Rendezvous, hell! There ain't been a real rendezvous up here in the mountains since 'forty or 'forty-two. You should'a seen 'em back in the shinin' times—"

"Shut up," Corrigan broke in. "I didn't ask for your life story, old man." He gestured with the pistol he held. "Get movin'. I want to get out of this cold weather before I freeze. Head on over there to that big buildin' that used to be the fur warehouse." He added to a couple of his men, "Get that stupid bastard we had to shoot and bring him along."

The rest of the outlaws closed in around Fargo, Maureen, and Dugan, and prodded them at gunpoint toward the warehouse. Fargo looked around and did a quick head count of the gang, allowing for the ones who had gone to fetch Milo. One man was missing and presumably dead or badly wounded, Fargo decided, brought down by either him or Dugan. The emigrants outnumbered the gang, but not by enough to overcome the disadvantage of being unarmed. The lack of weapons made all the difference in the world.

A groaning Milo was dragged from behind a wagon and shoved toward the other captives. He limped heavily from a bullet wound in his leg. As he came up to Fargo, he muttered, "I'm sorry I didn't keep Maureen inside."

She was still crying a little, but she sniffled and said, "No, Skye, it's all my fault. When I heard your rifle go off, I was afraid you'd been hurt. With that thing—"

Fargo's hand tightened on her arm, bringing a gasp from her and making her stop what she was saying. "Be careful," Fargo told her. "With all that snow on the ground, you can't see the rocks. You're liable to trip."

He glanced over at Milo and Dugan, a look of warning in his eyes. It might be too dark for them to see it; Fargo didn't know. But he had tried. And Maureen must have understood what he had been trying to tell her, because she said, "Yes, I almost stumbled just then."

Somewhere out there in the night was the Lost River Lurker, Fargo thought. His earlier wish that he could set the Lurker on Corrigan's gang was still haunting him. Dugan had said that the Lurker wouldn't leave the vicinity until he—or it—had revenge for being cut by Fargo's Arkansas toothpick. So far, except during its early morning encounter with Maureen, the Lurker had shown a great deal of savagery and ferocity. It had killed the guard and viciously attacked Fargo and Milo. If it came upon the outlaws, it might do some significant damage to them before they were able to kill it. Not only that, but the distraction that such an attack would provide might give Fargo and the others a chance to get their hands on some guns. If that happened, things could change in a hurry. Fargo didn't want Corrigan to have any warning that there could be more danger lurking— so to speak—in the darkness.

A bleak smile touched Fargo's mouth for a second. If anyone had told him that morning that before the next night was over he would be betting his life, and the lives of all his companions, on some sort of monster, he would have said the whole idea was crazy and impossible.

But after everything that had happened tonight, he wasn't sure he would ever believe that anything was impossible again.

A couple of Corrigan's men went ahead to open the big door into the warehouse. They stopped before they got there, and one of them turned to say, "There's a fire in there, Vince. I can see it through the gaps between the logs. Somebody must be inside."

"Probably just the rest of those dumb pilgrims," Corrigan said. "We took all their guns earlier. There's nothing to be afraid of, Griffith. Open the damned door."

Both men looked hesitant, but the one called Griffith grasped the rope latch and pulled the door back. Several members of the gang crowded forward at Corrigan's barked order, bristling with pistols and rifles. Fargo heard frightened cries and curses from those gathered inside the building.

Corrigan laughed. "Just like I thought. The whole pathetic bunch, huddled up like a flock of chickens." He shoved Milo, who stumbled on his wounded leg and almost fell. "Get in there."

Fargo, Maureen, Milo, and Dugan trooped into the warehouse. The light from the fire in the center of the large room showed Fargo the fear and disappointment on the faces of the emigrants. They had been counting on him to get them out of this mess, and yet he was a prisoner, and so were they. The outlaws spread out around the group, menacing them with their guns.

"I'll bet you folks didn't expect to ever see me again," Corrigan greeted them. "It would have been all right with me if I'd never set eyes on your ugly faces again. But here we are, and I reckon it's a good thing. We couldn't carry off all your supplies, so you brought what you had left to us."

"What you didn't steal from us, you mean!" Milo said, unable to contain his anger. "You're nothing but a damned thief!"

Corrigan smiled at him, said, "I never claimed any different," and then swung the revolver in his hand at Milo's head. Maureen cried out as the barrel thudded into the skull of her former brother-in-law and knocked him off his feet. He dropped to his knees.

"I don't want any more sass from you people," Corrigan said. Now that they were inside where the fire gave some light, Fargo got a better look at the outlaw leader. Corrigan was tall and lean and wore a long buckskin coat and a high-crowned hat with silver decorations around the band. Curly, light brown hair fell down the back of his neck and onto his shoulders. His face was narrow, and his mouth seemed set in a perpetual sneer. He had a hawk nose that had been broken in the past. In the dark eyes above it, Fargo saw cunning, rather than true intelligence, and something else that made him think of a diamondback rattlesnake. Corrigan's eyes were cold and almost as lifeless as glass, but Fargo suspected they had the capacity to hold an almost limitless amount of evil and cruelty.

Corrigan proved that by continuing, "All you women and girls, move over there on that side of the building. Men and boys over yonder on the other side." He grinned. "It's a mighty cold night, and it'll be colder by mornin'. I don't know any better way to keep warm than by cuddlin' with some pretty little gal."

8

Cries of outrage rose from the men in the group, along with whimpers of fear from the women. "Shut up that caterwaulin'!" Corrigan bellowed. "Do what I tell you, or I'll start shootin' the men, one by one! I don't have any use for them, and I can spare the bullets, by God!"

"Better do as he says," Fargo told the frightened group of emigrants. It pained him to tell them to go along with Corrigan, but if they didn't, there might well be a bloodbath here in a matter of moments.

Slowly, grudgingly, the emigrants sorted themselves out, men going one way, women the other. Corrigan ordered that the children had to go with the men, which meant that several infants began to wail as they were separated from their mothers. The older children cried, too, but silently for the most part.

"If you molest those women, there won't be any place west of the Mississippi where you'll ever be safe again, Corrigan," Fargo said quietly to the outlaw leader.

Corrigan chuckled. "You're mighty full of threats for a man who ain't goin' anywhere, Fargo."

"I'm not talking just about me. You'll be a marked man, and you know it. Not even the worst sorts will put up with a man who harms women."

"I ain't worried," Corrigan said flatly, with a shake of his head, and that told Fargo all he needed to know. There was no doubt now in Fargo's mind that Corrigan didn't intend to leave here until all of his prisoners were dead, right down to the youngest of the children.

In a way, that simplified things. If Fargo got the chance to kill Corrigan, he would do it without hesitation, treating the outlaw the same way he would a mad dog.

Of course, the way things stood now, he was a long way from having that chance . . .

Even some of Corrigan's men looked a bit leery of what their leader had in mind. One of them—the man called Griffith, Fargo thought—said, "I ain't sure this is a good idea, Vince . . ."

Corrigan turned on him angrily. "Who led these greenhorns right to you like pigs to the slaughter?" he demanded. "Who came up with the idea in the first place? I'm the one who does the thinkin' around here, not any of you boys. If you don't want to have a little fun, that's your own choice, but you ain't tellin' *me* what to do!"

Hurriedly, Griffith said, "Naw, I'd never try to do that, Vince. You got me all wrong."

Corrigan grunted in satisfaction. "I thought so." He swung back toward his captives. "Now . . . let me just see here . . ." Suddenly, he jabbed his gun toward a girl about sixteen years old with blond hair and a pretty, heart-shaped face. "You there! Come here to me, sweetheart."

The girl's face was streaked with tears already, and she started crying harder as she shook her head. The woman next to her put her arms around the girl's shoulders. Her hair was shorter, with gray mixed in among the blond, but the resemblance between mother and daughter was strong. "Leave her alone," the woman said to Corrigan. "Take me instead."

Corrigan laughed. With mocking politeness, he said, "No offense, missus, but not hardly. You look a mite stringy, especially compared to that gal of yours. I like my chickens a little more plump."

One of the men across the room shouted, "You son of a bitch!"

Corrigan twisted around sharply, his gun coming up

to point at the man responsible for the outburst. Behind him, both the woman and the girl screamed in fear.

Corrigan's face was drawn tight and had lines of hate and madness etched on it. His voice shaking a little, he said, "That pretty little gal gonna be without a daddy in about two seconds, and that wife o' yours is gonna be a widow."

The other men around the one who had cried out flinched away from him. It was only human nature; they couldn't help wanting to get out of the line of fire.

"P-please don't shoot him!" the girl said. "I'll do whatever you want, mister. Just please d-don't shoot him."

Fargo stood there, battling the urge to throw himself at Corrigan in a flying tackle. If he did that, somebody would let off a shot, sure as hell, and Fargo had a feeling that once a trigger was pulled in this tense atmosphere, the room would erupt in violence that wouldn't stop until all the emigrants were dead.

The angry look on Corrigan's face disappeared abruptly, to be replaced by an ugly grin. "You see, mister," he said to the man he was menacing with his gun, "that gal's mighty fond of you. She's willin' to do just about anything to save your hide." He kept the gun pointed at the man as he started to back toward the women. Without taking his eyes off the girl's father, he asked her, "What's your name, sweetheart?"

She had to swallow twice before she could answer, and even then it came out in a choked voice. "M-Maggie. Margaret."

"Well, Miss Maggie Margaret, is that fella over there with the big mouth your daddy?"

"Y-yes."

"And you love your daddy, don't you?"

"Yes."

"You just come on around here in front of me, Miss Maggie Margaret. Come on, don't be shy."

The girl pulled away from her mother's clutching embrace and moved slowly, fearfully, around Corrigan.

"Don't get between my gun and your pa," he warned her. "I'd sure hate to accidentally put a bullet between those pretty blue eyes of yours . . . That's good, right there." Corrigan's grin widened. "Now get down on your knees."

"Vince . . ." one of the other outlaws said. Their guns were steady as they covered the prisoners, but more than one man had a worried look on his face. "Vince, this ain't right."

"Shut up!" Corrigan snarled, his grin vanishing again. "Just shut your damn mouth and keep an eye on them pilgrims." He looked at the girl and said in a voice that was almost gentle, "I told you to get down on your knees."

Fargo looked at Maureen, Milo, and Dugan. He saw the same determination in all three sets of eyes. They were ready to jump Corrigan and his men, even though it was hopeless. They couldn't just stand by and watch what Corrigan was about to do. But they were looking to Fargo for their cue. They would follow his lead, even if it meant dying.

"On your knees," Corrigan repeated to the girl.

Outside, the most awful shriek Fargo had ever heard ripped through the night.

Corrigan jerked around, and the gun in his fist exploded as he involuntarily squeezed the trigger. The bullet grazed the neck of one of his own men, who yelped in pain and dropped his gun to grab at his neck. The slug thudded into the log wall.

Fargo grabbed Maureen, ready to throw her to the hard-packed dirt floor if the rest of the gang started shooting. But Corrigan shouted, "Hold your fire! No shootin', damn it!"

The shriek from outside had died away, leaving the big room gripped by an eerie silence. After a moment, one of Corrigan's men asked in a hushed voice, "What the hell was *that*?"

"Sounded like a . . . a panther," one of the other outlaws suggested.

Griffith shook his head. "Not like any panther I ever heard. It didn't even sound like an animal to me."

"Well, it sure as hell wasn't human," the other man shot back.

"Shut up!" Corrigan snapped. "Somebody go out there and see what that was."

None of the outlaws moved.

The girl called Maggie had taken advantage of the distraction to slip back over to her mother and the rest of the women. Corrigan seemed to have forgotten about her. Like everyone else in the warehouse, he had been taken by surprise by the scream, and shocked by it as well. Now, as none of his men budged to obey his command, his face darkened with anger and frustration.

"Blast it, I said for somebody to go see what that was!" he burst out. He jabbed his pistol at a couple of the men. "Griffith, you and Myers go. Now!"

"I ain't sure about this, Vince . . ." Griffith said slowly.

Corrigan leveled his revolver, aiming between Griffith's eyes. "Well, then, be sure of this," he snarled. "You get out there, or I'll blow your damned brains out!"

Griffith's face hardened, and for a second Fargo thought the man was going to turn his gun on Corrigan. Other than the danger to the emigrants from stray bullets, a falling-out between the outlaws was one of the best things Fargo could wish for at this point. He waited tensely to see what was going to happen, in hopes that he could turn it to his advantage. But then a grimace crossed Griffith's face, and he shrugged.

"Come on, Myers," he said. "Let's go."

The shriek hadn't been repeated, but that didn't mean that whatever had uttered it was gone. It could still be out there . . . lurking. Fargo glanced at Dugan and saw the minuscule nod the old trapper gave him. Dugan knew just as well as Fargo that the cry had come from the Lost River Lurker.

Griffith and Myers went to the door. Myers hesitated, then pulled it open. A little snow swirled in, but not

97

much. The two desperadoes stepped out, closing the door behind them.

Fargo's eyes swept the room. Nine outlaws left, including Corrigan. The prisoners outnumbered them more than two to one. But too many of that number were women and children, and there was still the matter of being unarmed. The odds needed to be whittled down some more before any sort of move against the outlaws would have a chance of succeeding.

Except for some sobs from the children, the room was quiet. The silence was strained by anticipation as everyone listened, expecting—maybe even fearing—that they would hear something else from outside.

When it came it was fast, a burst of gunshots from a pair of revolvers, followed immediately by screaming. Unlike the earlier cry, these shrieks were all too clearly human, the terrified screams of men in pain. After only a few seconds, both men abruptly fell silent. One was cut off in midscream; the other's cry died away in a bubbling gurgle. The dead silence that followed was somehow even more hideous.

Fargo looked at Corrigan. The outlaw leader was blinking furiously, and Fargo could almost see the wheels going around in his brain. Corrigan was scared, and he didn't know what to do. The more men he sent out of the warehouse, the greater the chance that the captives would revolt. Corrigan had to be aware of that. And yet, there was something out there, something awful, and it had issued a challenge, shrieking out its defiance and then killing Griffith and Myers. Fargo had no doubt the two outlaws were dead. He had fought the Lurker, had felt its strength and smelled its foulness, and he was confident that Griffith and Myers stood no chance against the creature, whatever it was.

Corrigan lifted his free hand and drew the back of it across his mouth. The hand shook a little as he did so. "All right," he said. "I don't hear nothin' else. I reckon it left."

"But Vince, what about Griffith and Myers?" one of the gang asked. "They ain't come back."

"They probably went to check on the horses. They'll be back after a while."

The words sounded hollow to Fargo, and they must have to everyone else, too. But no one wanted to argue with Corrigan, not the prisoners and not his own men. A few of the outlaws muttered to themselves, though, as they turned their attention back to the group of emigrants.

Corrigan gestured with his gun. "All of you pilgrims huddle up together. I ain't in the mood for fun anymore. Come morning, we'll figure out what to do with you."

Fargo had a pretty good idea he knew what Corrigan was planning. The men and boys and the younger children would be marched out and executed. The women and girls would remain prisoners until Corrigan was tired of them and their turn to die came. After what had just happened, though, Corrigan wasn't going to do anything that involved leaving the warehouse until daylight came.

That gave him some time, Fargo thought. A handful of hours to come up with a way to save not only his own life, but the lives of all these innocent emigrants as well.

It remained silent outside as the prisoners mingled together and were herded by the gunmen into a bunch by the rear wall. Fargo sat down with his back against the logs, Maureen on one side of him, Dugan on the other. As Milo sat down on the other side of Maureen, she said to him, "Let me look at your leg."

"It's all right," Milo insisted. His hand was pressed to the bloodstain on the leg of his trousers. "Just a flesh wound."

"Let me see it," Maureen said again.

Milo muttered something and moved his hand. Fargo leaned forward enough to watch as Maureen examined the wound. "It's just a graze," Milo said. "The bullet tore out a chunk of meat as it went by, but it didn't really go through my leg."

"You're lucky," Maureen said. "But it's still bleeding. It needs to be tied up." She raised her dress and tore a strip of fabric from the bottom of her petticoat. Working with deft fingers, she bandaged Milo's leg, tying the cloth tightly around the wound.

"Feels better already," Milo said through gritted teeth.

"Too bad you ain't got no whiskey to pour over it," Dugan put in. "That would keep it from festerin'."

Corrigan had assigned several of the outlaws to stand guard over the prisoners. He and the rest of the gang moved to the other side of the warehouse to sit down, eat some food they took from their packs, and pass around a bottle. The guards stood near the prisoners with their guns drawn, watching the emigrants more as a group than paying much attention to individuals. Fargo waited until Maureen was finished tending to Milo's leg, then said to her, "Change places with me."

"What?"

Milo glared across her at Fargo. "I'm fine the way things are now."

"Don't argue, just do it," Fargo said. "Milo, look unhappy about it."

"I *am* unhappy."

Maureen hesitated and then stood up, drawing the attention of the guards. She stepped across Fargo's legs as he moved closer to Milo, who drew back with a hostile frown. Maureen sat down on Fargo's other side, and he immediately put his arm around her shoulders and drew her closer to him. Milo's face grew even darker and angrier. Seeing that there wasn't going to be any sort of escape attempt, the guards lost interest and fell back into their half-bored stance. From time to time one of them glanced at the door, and the worried looks they gave it told Fargo they were still thinking about Griffith and Myers and whatever was out there that had made that awful noise.

Fargo kissed Maureen on the head as she snuggled against him, and then, without looking at the man on his other side, he hissed, "Milo!"

"What the hell do you want?" Milo responded.

"Take it easy. There's a reason for all this." Fargo was still looking down at Maureen, and to the guards it would appear that he was murmuring to her, rather than to her former brother-in-law. "Look away like you're mad, but keep listening."

A second passed in which Fargo didn't know if Milo understood what was going on, but then Milo said, "All right."

Fargo waited for a few moments, letting the guards see that he and Milo practically had their backs to each other in an attitude of open hostility. If the plan he was starting to hatch was going to have any chance of succeeding, the outlaws couldn't know that he and Milo had worked it out together. Finally, Fargo said, "Maureen, Dugan, you listen, too."

Maureen's head moved against Fargo's shoulder in a tiny nod. Dugan seemed to be staring straight ahead, but his eyes cut over to Fargo briefly and told the Trailsman that the old-timer had heard.

"We've got to cut the odds down before morning," Fargo went on. "The best way to do that is to get more of those outlaws to go outside, so the thing that's out there can do our work for us. Listen, Milo. Here's what I want you to do . . ."

Time dragged. More than an hour had passed since the prisoners were herded together again. Milo looked around. Beside him, both Fargo and Maureen appeared to have dozed off as they held each other. Milo scowled at them and got to his feet. One of the guards turned toward him, lifting his pistol. Milo held up his hands to show that he meant no harm as he limped slowly toward the guard.

"That's far enough, mister," the outlaw said, his voice sounding loud. It was quieter in the old warehouse now. Fargo and Maureen weren't the only ones who had gone to sleep. Most of the children and some of the adults had, too. Those still awake were sitting around holding each other, trying to draw strength from one another in this time of terror.

"Take it easy," Milo said. "I want to talk to Corrigan."

"You just go back over there and sit down," the guard said, gesturing with his gun. "The boss ain't got nothin' to say to you."

"I've got something to say to him," Milo insisted. "Something important."

On the other side of the warehouse, a few of the outlaws had gone to sleep, aided by the rotgut they had guzzled. Corrigan was still awake, though, and he came to his feet, uncoiling like a snake. "What's goin' on over there?" he called.

The guard turned his head. "This pilgrim wants to talk to you, Vince."

"It's important," Milo added. "Mighty important."

Corrigan hesitated, frowning as he thought. The fire in the center of the room had burned down, and the glare it cast over Corrigan's face was red, like the fires of hell. Finally Corrigan put his right hand on the butt of his gun and motioned with his left. "Come on over here, Haydon," he said. "But if you try anything, I'll kill you."

"No need for threats," Milo said as he shuffled toward Corrigan. "I'm looking for a way out of this, not for more trouble."

Fargo watched through a single slitted eye as Milo approached Corrigan. So far the plan was working. They were too far away for Fargo to be able to hear what was being said as Milo came to a stop in front of the outlaw leader, but he didn't have to hear. He knew the yarn that Milo was spinning. He had come up with most of it.

"Look, I know what you're planning to do to us," Milo said grimly to Corrigan. "Is there anything I can say to change your mind?"

Corrigan grinned. "Not likely."

"What if I told you I know where you can get a lot of money? Gold, greenbacks, silver . . . a damn fortune, Corrigan."

"How would you know anything like that?" Corrigan

asked with a shake of his head. "You're nothing but a stupid pilgrim."

"You just thought you found all the wagon train's money. You never found the real cache."

Corrigan stiffened. "What the hell are you talking about? I got that strongbox out of your wagon."

Milo leaned closer. "There's more," he whispered. "A lot more. And I'll tell you where to find it if you'll let me go."

Corrigan studied Milo intently for a long moment, then he asked, "What about the others?"

Milo cast a guilty glance over his shoulder. "I think you should let them go, too," he suggested, "but if you won't . . ."

"Then your own hide is all you really care about." Corrigan laughed. "You act so high-and-mighty, but you ain't really any different than anybody else. You look out for yourself, and devil take the hindmost."

Milo managed to look both ashamed of himself and angry at the same time. "What about it?" he demanded. "Are you interested or not, Corrigan?"

Corrigan slipped a knife from a sheath on his belt and ran the keen edge of the blade over the ball of his thumb. It sliced the skin but didn't go deep enough to draw blood. "Maybe you should just go ahead and tell me, and then we'll see whether or not I'm feelin' generous."

Milo shook his head. "What kind of fool do you take me for?"

"Look around and answer that for yourself."

Milo flushed but stayed in control of his temper. "No deal. Give me Fargo's horse, a gun, and some supplies, and I ride away from here. But not before I tell you where to find the loot."

"You'd really leave that sister-in-law of yours? I remember the way you used to look at her when she wasn't watchin'." Corrigan gave him a lecherous grin.

Milo glanced at the apparently sleeping Fargo and Maureen. "She made her choice," he said with a bitter edge in his voice. "If she wants Fargo so much, she can stay right here with him."

"Now I'm startin' to believe you, Haydon. I can understand a man who's lookin' to get a little vengeance on them that's wronged him." Corrigan brought the tip of the knife close to Milo's throat. "But I still want to know where that money is before I think about lettin' you go."

Milo's eyes cut downward at the knife. He swallowed and then inclined his head toward the door. "It's out there. In one of the wagons."

Corrigan shook his head. "Can't be. We searched all the wagons."

"You missed the hiding place, that's all. We were mighty careful about where we put it."

"You're lyin'," Corrigan snapped. He dug the point of the blade into Milo's neck, under the beard. Milo caught his breath in pain. Corrigan pulled the knife back. There was a spot of crimson blood on the tip. "Tell me the damn truth, or I'll shove this blade clean through your neck next time."

"It . . . it is the truth!" Milo said. "There's a false bed in one of the wagons. You can't find it unless you know where to look."

Milo's voice was loud enough now so that Fargo's keen ears picked up the words on the other side of the room. If he heard them, he was sure that the outlaws did, too. The way several heads swiveled toward Corrigan and Milo told Fargo that he was right.

"I still ain't sure I believe you," Corrigan said. "But I reckon we could have overlooked something like that."

"Are you gonna let me go now?"

"I'll think on it," Corrigan said with his evil grin. "Until I've made up my mind, you just go on back over there and sit down with your friends."

"You can't back out on it," Milo said. "We had a deal—"

"The hell we did! Go on now, before I get tired of tellin' you."

Milo looked like he was about to cry. "I told you the truth," he said. "I told you where to find the money."

"We'll see about that, come morning," Corrigan said.

With those words, Fargo felt his hopes sink. He wanted to get Corrigan or some of the other outlaws to leave the warehouse and go looking for that hidden money, which didn't really exist. If they did, chances were they would run into the Lurker. Despite not hearing any evidence of its presence for the past couple of hours, Fargo believed the thing was still close by.

But Corrigan hadn't taken the bait, and now all the captives had to look forward to was daybreak—and death.

9

Maureen whispered, "Oh, Skye, it didn't work!" Her hands clutched tighter at Fargo as she leaned against him. Together they watched Milo shuffling dispiritedly across the room toward them.

"Take it easy," Fargo told her. "Pretend we didn't see any of that. Act like you're still asleep."

Maureen burrowed her face against him, and he could tell that she was trying not to cry. It had been a long shot from the first, Fargo thought. He had counted on Corrigan's greed being strong enough to overcome his fear of whatever was out there in the dark. Not that Fargo had figured Corrigan himself would go to look for the money. His hope had been that the outlaw leader would send one or two of his men. Then when the Lurker got them, the odds would be that much better for the emigrants. Still not good, but better.

Sighing, Milo resumed his seat against the wall beside Fargo. He didn't say anything. No words were necessary to convey how he felt about the failure of the plan.

A short time later, Maureen's breathing deepened as she huddled against Fargo. Pretending to be asleep had given way to the real thing. Exhaustion had claimed her.

Fargo was still awake, though, his brain racing swiftly, coming up with ideas and then discarding them as he realized they were unworkable. This was one of the worst fixes he'd been in. But he wasn't ready to give up. Not with so many lives at stake.

After a while, he noticed that Corrigan hadn't returned to the other side of the room. He still stood by himself, his brow furrowed in thought. As Fargo watched, Corrigan took out the makin's and rolled a quirly, then lit it with a lucifer. He gazed meditatively toward the prisoners as he smoked.

A few minutes went by, and then Corrigan abruptly strode toward them. The guards snapped into alertness as their boss approached. The prisoners shrunk aside from Corrigan as if *he* were the monster. Maybe they weren't far wrong about that, Fargo thought as he lifted his head, opened his eyes fully, and watched Corrigan.

Corrigan came to a stop in front of Fargo and kicked his foot. "Get up."

Corrigan's voice roused Maureen from sleep. She blinked in confusion, looked up and saw Corrigan, and gasped in fear. Corrigan drew his gun.

"I said get up," he repeated to Fargo.

Fargo took his arm from around Maureen's shoulders and put a hand on the ground to brace himself as he climbed to his feet. He stood there, waiting silently, unsure what Corrigan had on his mind.

Corrigan jerked the gun at Milo. "You, too, Haydon."

"What the hell is this?" Milo demanded as he stood up.

"I been thinkin' about what you told me a while ago. About that money you pilgrims have got hidden. I want it, Haydon."

Milo shrugged. "Go out and get it, then."

Corrigan gave him a sly grin. "I reckon that's just what you want me to do. You want to send me out there so whatever got Griffith and Myers will get me."

He had figured out that much, anyway, Fargo thought. Corrigan was nothing if not cunning.

Corrigan shook his head and went on, "I ain't that stupid. But I want that money, so you're gonna go get it for me."

Fargo kept his face carefully expressionless. Corrigan hadn't fallen for the trick, but he did believe that Milo had been telling the truth about the money. Corrigan's greed wouldn't allow him to discard completely the possibility that the emigrants had cached the bulk of their money in the false bottom of a wagon. He had to check it out, or he wouldn't be able to live with himself.

That meant they still had a chance, Fargo told himself.

"I'm not going out there," Milo said. "Not until you promise to let me loose if I do what you want."

Corrigan raised his gun. "I could just wait until morning and have my boys tear every one of those wagons apart. But I'm the impatient sort. I want that money *now*. Unless you were lyin' to me, Haydon, in which case I'll just go ahead and kill you."

"Take it easy," Fargo said. He moved between Milo and Corrigan and faced Milo. "What the hell is he talking about? What hidden money?" Since Fargo had joined forces with the emigrants after Corrigan had robbed them, it would make sense that he knew nothing about the supposed cache. He had to keep playing his role perfectly, or Corrigan might tumble to the fact that they had made the whole thing up.

Milo grimaced and looked down at the ground. "We got quite a bit of cash hidden in a false bottom in one of the wagons."

Maureen spoke up, sounding outraged. "And you offered to trade that for your freedom? My God, Milo, what sort of man are you?"

"The sort who doesn't want to die here!" he flared at her. "I'm sorry, but that's the way I feel."

Corrigan chuckled. "Well, I don't reckon you ever had much chance with the lady, Haydon, but you sure as hell don't have any now. Not that I give a damn. Now, about that money . . ."

Fargo glanced around at the other members of the group. The children were still asleep, but most of the adults were awake. Some of them looked puzzled by this talk about money they knew to be nonexistent, but at least they all had the good sense to keep quiet. They seemed to understand that it was all a bluff, and Fargo hoped they would keep on acting just like they were.

He turned back to Corrigan. "We'll go get it for you."

"That's more like it. But don't think I'm crazy enough

to send the two of you out there all by your lonesome."
Corrigan turned his head. "Asa."

"I ain't goin' out there, Vince," replied the outlaw
he had spoken to. "Not after what happened to them
other boys."

"That's not what I want," Corrigan snapped. "Bring
me the old man's buffalo gun."

The outlaw got Dugan's Sharps from the pile of captured weapons and handed it to Corrigan, who took it
and said to Dugan, "Give me the shells for this cannon."

Grudgingly, Dugan pulled a pouch from under his
thick coat and tossed it to Corrigan. "I hope it blows up
in your face," he said.

"Not likely. Looks like you've taken good care of this
gun." Corrigan opened the breech, slipped one of the
heavy cartridges into it, and slapped it closed. "A Big
Fifty like this will knock a bull buffalo off its feet if you
hit it right. I reckon it'll knock down anything prowlin'
around outside." He grinned at Fargo and Milo. "And
it'll punch a mighty big hole through you if you try to
double-cross me."

So that was Corrigan's plan. He would cover them
with the Sharps from the door of the warehouse as they
went out to retrieve the money. If the Lurker jumped
them, or if they tried to make a break for it, Corrigan
would be ready to shoot.

Corrigan jabbed the barrel of the heavy carbine
toward the door. "Go on," he told Fargo and Milo. "I'm
tired of wastin' time."

The two men moved toward the doorway. Milo was
still limping from his wound, but not as badly now that
Maureen had bandaged it. One of the outlaws pulled the
door open, casting an apprehensive glance outside as he
did so. Nothing came out of the darkness except cold
air. Fargo paused for a second. He drew in a deep
breath, feeling the chilly bite of the air. He didn't smell
the distinctive stench of the Lurker. It had withdrawn
again after killing Griffith and Myers. But that didn't
mean it wasn't somewhere close by. It could be watching
them at this very moment.

"No lollygaggin' around," Corrigan warned them. "Get out there, get the money, and get back in here. I'll have my sights on you the whole time."

Fargo walked out into the snow with Milo behind him. Milo leaned closer and asked in a low voice, "What do we do now?"

"Make it look good," Fargo hissed. "Head for one of the wagons that's not too close. We'll need some distance."

He wasn't sure what he was going to do. The important thing was to get out from under Corrigan's gun and maybe get his hands on that pepperbox Dugan had told him was hidden in the cabin. Then they could try to draw out Corrigan with the rest of the outlaws. It would have to be done quickly, otherwise Corrigan would just threaten to shoot the women and children and force Fargo to surrender again.

And there was still a wild card to be played. A huge, incredibly strong, foul-smelling wild card . . .

Milo tramped up alongside Fargo and then drew ahead slightly. "It's that one over there," he said, loud enough for Corrigan to hear, as he pointed at the wagon parked the farthest from the warehouse. Fargo glanced over his shoulder and saw Corrigan just inside the door, silhouetted against the glow of the fire behind him. The boss outlaw had the Sharps leveled at Fargo and Milo.

"Ugh!" Milo said, stopping abruptly.

"What is it?" Fargo asked.

"Something strewn around on the ground up here. I think it's . . . guts."

Fargo moved up for a look. Milo was right. The Lurker had torn Griffith and Myers to pieces and left parts of them lying around.

"We'll go around them," Fargo said.

"Yeah." Milo's voice shook a little, but his step was steady enough, considering his limp, as he walked past the gruesome remains of one of the outlaws.

"Corrigan can shoot only one of us," Milo went on as they approached the wagon where the loot was supposed to be hidden. "When we get up here, we'll split up, fast.

You got to promise me, though, Fargo, that if you're the one who gets away, you'll do everything you can to get Maureen out of there."

"Sure. I know you'll do the same."

"Yeah," Milo said. "I'd never let anything bad happen to her if I could help it."

Some of that feeling came from guilt, Fargo knew, because Milo still blamed himself for his brother's death. And some came from Milo's own feelings for Maureen. Maybe someday, if the two of them survived this, they could get things straight between them. Fargo hoped it would all work out for the best.

That little matter of survival came first, though. They were almost at the wagon.

"I'll go left," Milo said. "You go right—"

The Lost River Lurker came straight ahead, leaping onto the wagon seat and then throwing himself at Fargo and Milo with an inhuman screech.

Fargo had caught a whiff of the creature's rancid smell just before the Lurker appeared, but that was the only warning he had. He flung himself to the side, but one of the Lurker's outspread arms caught him anyway, smacking him hard and spinning him around. Fargo felt himself falling and tumbled into the snow. He heard the heavy boom of the Sharps but had no idea if Corrigan's shot had hit the Lurker. Something that big might be hard to miss, even in the dark.

Fargo rolled over and surged to his feet, looking for both the Lurker and Milo. To his surprise, he saw a huge dark shape sprawled on the ground, motionless. Had Corrigan killed the Lurker? As the outlaw had said, those .50 caliber slugs thrown by the Sharps packed enough punch to knock down a buffalo.

There was no sign of Milo. Fargo wondered for an instant if the man was *under* the Lurker.

Then, with a throaty growl, the creature heaved itself up off the ground. Fargo had time to see that it hadn't crushed Milo when it fell, but then he had to throw himself aside in a desperate dive in order to avoid the Lurker's lunge. Fargo slid underneath the wagon.

That didn't stop the Lurker. The creature grabbed the bed of the vehicle and heaved. The wagon tipped up and over with a splintering of wheel spokes. The Sharps roared again, but this time Corrigan missed. Fargo heard the slug whine as it ricocheted off iron.

With the Lurker looming over him, Fargo had no place to run. He went on the attack instead, throwing himself at the thing's legs. He hoped his rolling tackle would knock the Lurker off its feet.

The Lurker didn't budge, and suddenly Fargo felt something grab hold of his legs. For a horrified instant he thought the Lurker was going to tear him in half like a wishbone, but then the creature flung him through the air with the ease of a child tossing aside an unwanted toy. Fargo tried to curl himself into a ball to lessen the impact of his landing, but he crashed to the ground with bone-jarring force. Only the thick layer of snow cushioned his fall and saved him from breaking his neck.

More guns were popping now. The rest of the gang had joined Corrigan at the entrance to the warehouse to throw lead at the monster. Some of them had spilled outside the building. They filled the air with bullets, so that Fargo was in as much danger of being shot as he was of having the Lurker rip him apart or twist his head off.

Fargo lifted his head and saw the Lurker shambling toward him. He heard bullets thudding into the creature's hairy hide, but they didn't seem to have any effect. Fargo came up on hands and knees and grabbed one of the broken wagon spokes from the ground. As the Lurker reached for him, he swung the makeshift club, slashing it across the creature's face. The Lurker hesitated. Fargo reversed the broken spoke and jabbed the jagged end at the beast as it rushed forward, arms spread wide to envelop him.

The shock of the blow shivered up Fargo's arms as he drove the broken spoke into the Lurker's body. That didn't stop the creature's charge. Fargo was picked up and hurled backward. Only a frantic flip to the side carried him out of the Lurker's path.

The fight had taken them behind the wagon, Fargo realized. Corrigan and the other outlaws couldn't see them anymore. And the Lurker was stumbling, finally slowed a bit by all the damage it had taken. Fargo seized the opportunity.

He turned and ran.

Boots weren't the best footwear for running. Fargo wished he had his moccasins, despite the cold and snow. Even wearing boots, though, he was able to outrun the Lurker. He dashed behind another wagon. As he did so, he heard Corrigan yell, "Where the hell's Fargo? Get out there and find him!"

A grin tugged fleetingly at Fargo's mouth. None of the outlaws would want to venture too far from the warehouse with the Lurker around, no matter how scared they were of Corrigan.

Fargo looked back. The Lurker had stopped chasing him and was tearing up the canvas cover of the over-turned wagon instead. Corrigan shot at it again with the Sharps. The Lurker turned and reached the log wall of the stockade in a couple of bounds. Like a lizard, he seemed to slither up the wall and was gone.

That made Fargo's next moves more urgent. Without the threat of the Lurker to hold them back, the outlaws would be after him. In fact, Corrigan was still yelling at them, telling them to go find both him and Milo.

Fargo wondered what had happened to Milo. The man was out here somewhere in the darkness. The Lurker might have killed him, though Fargo didn't think there had been time for the creature to do that. How long did it take, though, to yank a man's head off his shoulders? Not long at all, Fargo thought grimly.

The wagons provided cover for him until he almost reached the cabins. He had to dash across open ground and was spotted by one of the bandits.

"There he goes!"

"You sure it wasn't that monster?" another man called.

"I think it was Fargo!"

Fargo reached the nearest cabin and flattened himself

against a side wall. He worked his way around to the back. If he was remembering right, Ed Dugan's cabin was three buildings over. Fargo had to reach that cabin, get inside, and remove that pepperbox from its hiding place.

He stayed in the deep shadows behind the cabins, moving one way while the men seeking him came from the opposite direction and in front. Fargo tried to time his dashes from cabin to cabin so that he wouldn't be spotted, and the fact that no more outcries arose told him that he was so far successful.

He reached the rear of Dugan's cabin. His heart was thudding in his chest. The only way into the cabin was by the front door, and when he tried to get to it, he would be out in the open again and easily spotted. Corrigan's men would rush to the cabin. Fargo might have time to retrieve the hidden pepperbox, but what good would a little gun like that do against several heavily armed opponents?

Still, it was his only chance. Fargo leaned against the chimney for a moment, catching his breath before he made his attempt.

The chimney moved.

Fargo jerked away, startled. The chimney was constructed of rocks and attached to the rear wall, and the last thing it should have done was move. He put his hand on it and pushed hard. The chimney shifted again. Not much, but it definitely moved.

But only one section of it, Fargo now saw as his hands began to explore. One side of the chimney was hinged. It pushed in a couple of inches and then stopped, unable to go any farther. Fargo ran his hands over the face of the chimney wall. His fingers slipped into holes that had been drilled in the rock. He hung on and pulled. The chimney wall moved on its hidden hinges and swung outward.

A dark opening loomed before him. He smelled ashes and charred wood.

He hadn't looked down at the ground before, but he

did so now and saw marks in the snow that indicated this hidden door had been opened recently. There were other marks that could have been the vestiges of footprints. Suddenly Fargo knew how the Lurker had gotten into and out of the cabin the morning Maureen had seen it. Having witnessed the results of the creature's ferocity and experienced it firsthand as well, Fargo knew that Maureen was lucky to be alive. Evidently, the Lurker had been in a curious mood at that moment, rather than being gripped by the killing rage that seemed to be its more common state.

Whenever a big fire was burning in the fireplace, this means of entrance to the cabin would be blocked. But when the fire had died down or was out, a person would be able to slide through the opening, crouch low, slip around the hearth, and step out. Having seen the Lurker absorb several bullets tonight, Fargo had a hunch that a little fire wouldn't bother the creature very much.

By this time, the fire that Dugan had burning earlier was just embers. Fargo slid through the hidden door, used similar finger holds on the inside to pull it closed behind him, and stepped into the cabin. As big as the Lurker was, this was probably a tight fit for him, but he could make it. His encounter with Maureen was proof enough of that.

Dugan had left a candle burning. It was almost melted down, but its tiny flame still flickered and provided enough illumination for Fargo to find the rock he was looking for. He started at the upper left corner of the fireplace, counted down five rocks, then over three. The rock was loose, though it would look just as solid as all the others to anyone who didn't know about the hiding place. Fargo wiggled it back and forth and worked it out, reached into the dark hole behind it. His fingers closed around the butt of the pepperbox pistol.

He pulled it out in the light and saw that it was a Marston, with a four-inch, six-barrel cluster and was fully loaded. Something was engraved in the wooden grip. Fargo's fingers felt the markings. He held the gun at an angle to the poor light and peered at it. The engraving was worn, but the words were still legible. A name: *Arthur Dugan.*

Fargo frowned. Who was Arthur Dugan? The old trapper's first name was Ed. Maybe Arthur was Ed's brother, Fargo decided. He was curious, but the answer was really unimportant now. What mattered was that he was no longer unarmed.

The short barrel of the Marston made it wildly inaccurate at distances over a few feet, and the .31 caliber slugs didn't possess much stopping power. Still, Fargo felt a lot better for having it. Since he was unsure how long the gun had been cached here, all he could do was hope that the caps and the powder charges were still good. A misfire at the wrong time could ruin everything.

He went to the door of the cabin and eased it open an inch or two. He heard the voices of Corrigan's men calling out to each other as they searched for him. One sounded close as the outlaw said, "I'll look in this one."

Fargo knew the man was talking about this cabin. He pulled the door shut silently and darted over to the candle to blow it out, plunging the room into stygian darkness. Then he pressed his back against the wall to one side of the door.

The outlaw used the barrel of his rifle to shove the door open and then came through in a rush, sweeping the rifle from side to side to cover the whole room—except for the area behind him, on either side of the door. Fargo stepped up and pressed the barrels of the pepperbox to the back of the man's neck.

"Don't move!" Fargo hissed. "If I fire all six of these barrels at once, the blast'll blow right through your spine and tear your throat out."

The outlaw had stiffened into immobility at the touch of the gun's cold steel. He managed to say, "D-don't shoot me, mister!"

"Hold your rifle out to your left side," Fargo ordered.

The man did so, and Fargo reached out with his left hand and plucked it from the man's grip. As soon as he had the rifle, he pulled the pepperbox away from the outlaw's neck and smashed the butt of the rifle against it instead. The outlaw grunted in pain and fell to his knees, then pitched forward onto his face, stunned.

Fargo knelt and found the man's pistol, slipped it out of its holster. The revolver was a Colt, much like Fargo's own. He slid it into his empty holster and stood up, still holding the pepperbox. He turned toward the door.

Another dark figure appeared, coming toward him. Before Fargo had a chance to do anything else, the newcomer yelled, "Hey! You ain't Quint!" He started to bring up the rifle in his hands.

Fargo squeezed the trigger of the pepperbox. The little pistol fired, and at this distance, the second outlaw was flung backward by the impact of all six .31 caliber bullets smashing into his chest. His rifle cracked as he involuntarily jerked the trigger in dying, but the barrel was already pointing skyward.

That would draw plenty of attention, Fargo knew. At least he was much better armed and better able to deal with trouble now. He darted out of the cabin and ran toward the parked wagons as more of the outlaws began to shout questions and hurry toward the sound of the shots.

Now the real work began. It was time to whittle down the odds until the only outlaw left was Corrigan. He and Fargo would face each other for the final showdown. Fargo was looking forward to that.

He reached the wagons and crouched behind the closest. A gust of wind whipped snow around him. As the snow settled back toward the ground, the scene around Fargo grew brighter. He looked up at the sky and saw that the clouds were parting in places, allowing more starlight to shine through. Morning was still a few hours away, and by the time it arrived, the sky might well be clear. If the wind died down before then, the temperature would plummet. The morning could be the coldest one this season.

That was what Fargo was thinking when he heard the soft scrape of a footstep close behind him and threw himself to the side to avoid the blow that swept down at his head.

10

Something—a club of some sort—grazed Fargo's left shoulder, just hard enough to make his arm go numb for a second. He had the outlaw's rifle in his right hand. He drove it forward as he twisted around, jabbing the barrel hard into the belly of the man who had just attacked him. The man grunted, *"Ooof!"* and doubled over, dropping the club. Something about his voice was familiar. Fargo grabbed his shoulder, jerked him upright, and shoved the barrel of the rifle under his chin. He could see the jutting beard now.

"Milo?" Fargo rasped.

"Y-yeah. Fargo? Is that you?"

Fargo let go of him and stepped back. "You damned fool," he said quietly. "I could have blown your head off."

"Yeah, well, you nearly got your skull stove in," Milo replied. "I thought you were one of Corrigan's men." He paused, then added, "Where'd you get the rifle?"

"From one of them. Where have you been since the Lurker jumped us?"

"Hiding. Looking for something I could use as a weapon. Never found anything except an old branch."

"The Lurker didn't come after you?"

"No, he was too busy trying to rip you limb from limb. I crawled off under the wagons, been laying low ever since. I thought a time or two that one of those outlaws was going to find me, but none of them did. Then I saw someone, thought I'd take a risk to get my hands on a gun."

Fargo held out the rifle. "Here, take this one. I've got a Colt, too."

Milo took the weapon and said, "That feels a lot better. We going after Corrigan now?"

"There are still too many of them," Fargo said. "I'd like to take care of a few more before we risk that."

"Yeah, I reckon you're right." Milo sounded a little disappointed. "I'd sure like to get that son of a bitch in my sights, though."

"You and me both," Fargo said. He held up a hand for silence. Low-pitched voices were coming toward them.

"—no sign of it now, whatever it was."

"Looked like a bear to me."

"I never saw no bear that could move like that. Nor any other kind of animal."

"You sayin' it was a man who tore up poor old Griffith and Myers like that?"

"I'm sayin' I'll be damned glad to get back behind some sturdy log walls again," the first man declared. "I don't much care whether Fargo and that other fella get away. What can they do to us? There's only two of 'em."

"Yeah, but Fargo's got Quint's rifle and pistol. Vince ain't gonna be satisfied until he's skinned Fargo and pinned his hide to the wall."

The two outlaws had come even with the wagon where Fargo and Milo were waiting. Fargo looked at Milo and nodded, and as the two outlaws walked past, they struck quickly, darting out behind the men. Milo slammed the stock of the rifle against one man's head, while Fargo reversed the Colt and used the butt of it to lay out the other. Both desperadoes dropped like poleaxed steers.

Fargo holstered the Colt and hauled one senseless outlaw behind the wagon. Milo did the same with the other man. When the unconscious bodies were concealed, Milo searched them for weapons. He came up with two more rifles, two pistols, and a knife. He gave one of the rifles to Fargo and tucked both pistols behind his belt.

Then, before Fargo realized what he was doing, Milo leaned over, and with starlight glittering on the knife blade, he cut the throats of both men with swift, back and forth strokes.

Fargo's hand gripped Milo's arm. "What the hell did you do that for?"

"I didn't want them waking up and coming up behind us later on," Milo said. "Besides, the sons of bitches deserved it. They rode with Corrigan, didn't they?"

Fargo shared his companion's loathing for Vince Corrigan and his gang, but the Trailsman's innate sense of justice and fair play balked at cold-blooded murder, no matter the justification. "Next time, we'll just tie them up and gag them," he said. "Give me the knife."

Milo shrugged and handed over the blade, clearly not bothered by Fargo's disapproval.

If Fargo was counting right, Corrigan had only half a dozen men left, including the one Fargo had knocked out in Dugan's cabin. That man probably had come to his senses by now. Corrigan made seven. Seven to two wasn't good odds, but they were a lot better than they had been earlier in the night, especially considering that Fargo and Milo were now well armed. In fact, they were on the verge of being walking arsenals, Fargo thought as they started circling the interior of the stockade, working their way toward the warehouse where Corrigan still held the rest of the emigrants.

With all those lives at stake, Fargo and Milo couldn't just burst into the warehouse and start shooting, even assuming that such a tactic would prove effective against Corrigan and his gang. The chance was too great that a stray bullet would hit one of the innocents.

"Whatever happened to that monster?" Milo asked in a whisper as they crept along the fence.

"It lit out," Fargo replied, "after being shot a few times."

"I heard that buffalo gun of Dugan's go off. Did Corrigan hit the thing with that?"

"I think so."

"And that didn't kill it?" Milo's voice was full of wonder and a little fear. "I didn't think there was anything one of those Big Fifties couldn't kill."

Fargo didn't say anything. He wondered if the Lost River Lurker had crawled off to die from its wounds. From what he had seen of the thing, he wouldn't be surprised if it had a lair around here, a cave in a hillside, maybe. It might live like a bear, whether it really was one or not.

He hoped they had seen the last of the Lurker. Dealing with Corrigan and the rest of the outlaws would be hard enough. If Fargo could have counted on the creature to attack only Corrigan's men, that would be different. But the Lurker was wild and unpredictable, and if it served as an ally to Fargo's cause, it would be by accident.

As they neared the warehouse, Fargo lifted a hand to signal a halt. He went to one knee in the snow and motioned for Milo to do likewise. As they knelt there, Fargo leaned close to the other man and whispered, "We still need to draw Corrigan out of there. The farther away he and his men are from the others, the better."

Milo nodded his agreement. "Got any ideas?"

Fargo glanced up at the sky. The clouds had thinned even more, allowing starlight and the faint illumination from a slice of moon to fall over the old fort. But the night was still dark, too dark to make out many details. At a distance, a man would be visible as only a dark shadow against the white of the snow.

"Yeah, I've got an idea," Fargo said. "You're going to take me prisoner."

"What?" Milo asked, startled.

Quickly, Fargo explained his plan. Milo listened, then nodded dubiously.

"It might work," he admitted. "But it's one hell of a risk."

"Yeah," Fargo said, "but so is everything else in life."

Milo couldn't argue with that. He said, "Let's get to it."

They moved toward the front of the warehouse. Milo

tugged his hat down so that the upper half of his face was covered. A couple of Corrigan's men had beards, Fargo had noticed, so that wouldn't give Milo's identity away immediately. Fargo took the Colt from his holster and slipped it under his belt in the small of his back. When they were positioned where they wanted to be, he laid the rifle on the ground in front of him. Then Milo jabbed the barrel of the other rifle in his back.

"Vince!" Milo shouted, loud enough to be heard inside the warehouse. "Vince, I got him! I got Fargo!"

Milo made his voice hoarse, almost unrecognizable. Fargo's hope was that Corrigan would be so eager to see the Trailsman captured that he wouldn't take the time to worry too much about which of his men had accomplished that goal.

Fargo lifted his hands to shoulder level and hung his head in an air of abject defeat as the door of the warehouse flew open. A slanted rectangle of light spilled through the open doorway, reaching almost to Fargo's boots. Corrigan stepped out, saying, "It's damned well about time!"

Milo took the rifle barrel away from Fargo's back and raised the weapon, then smashed the butt of it against Fargo's neck. That was what it looked like, anyway. The blow was hard enough to sting a little, but Milo pulled most of the force at the last second. Fargo pitched forward, facedown in the snow, as if Milo had just clouted the hell out of him.

When he landed, his hand closed over the rifle he had placed there a few moments earlier. He lay still, as if stunned.

"Hold on!" Corrigan yelled as he strode out of the warehouse followed by several of his men. "I want to kill the son of a bitch myself!"

Fargo watched through slitted eyes as the boss outlaw advanced. He tried to count the men who came with Corrigan, but it was difficult from this angle. And some of the outlaws were still wandering around the fort, too, searching for Fargo and Milo. Those men would be converging on this spot now, though, having been drawn in by the commotion. There couldn't be more than one or two men left in the warehouse, Fargo decided. It was even possible there were none.

Corrigan was only about fifteen feet away now. He would realize at any second that Milo wasn't really one of his men. The time had come, Fargo thought. He couldn't afford to wait any longer.

He came up out of the snow, bringing the rifle with him. He was going to shout for Corrigan to surrender, but the outlaw didn't give him a chance. Corrigan howled, "It's a trick!" and jerked his gun from its holster.

Fargo fired as Corrigan tried to get a shot off. The bullet smacked into Corrigan and spun him around, driving him off his feet. Fargo worked the lever of the rifle and squeezed off another shot as Milo opened fire. Fargo's second bullet doubled up another outlaw with a belly wound, and Milo's shot blew the legs out from under another man.

The outlaws were fighting back, though. Muzzle flashes ripped through the darkness and gun blasts echoed over the snow. Bullets whipped around Fargo's head. He went to the side in a rolling dive. Milo went the other way. As Fargo came up on his knees, he saw a figure rushing at him out of the night. He pulled the trigger, firing the rifle one-handed. The outlaw charging toward him was flung backward by the bullet that drove into his body.

Fargo surged to his feet. A couple of bounds put him behind a wagon. He took a deep breath of the cold air, then edged an eye around the corner of the wagon bed to look at the area in front of the warehouse. He didn't see Milo anywhere, but he didn't call out to see if he was all right. If Milo had sought cover, as Fargo suspected he had, he didn't want to give away his position.

As Fargo focused on the area in front of the warehouse where the light from the open door fell, he bit back a curse. Corrigan was gone. The wound he had suffered hadn't been enough to keep him on the ground. Fargo hoped Corrigan hadn't made it back inside the warehouse. He might be furious enough to start slaughtering the emigrants.

A burst of shots came from the vicinity of a cabin. Either the outlaws had found Milo, or they had gotten trigger-happy and were shooting at each other in the darkness. That was certainly possible, but Fargo knew he couldn't count on it.

He had to get into the warehouse to protect Maureen and the other people in there. He would have to cross quite a bit of open ground to reach the door, however, and would be an easy target for any outlaws who were behind cover, their rifles lined on the doorway.

So he had to make them look somewhere else, and he could think of only one way to do that. He reached inside the wagon, feeling around for a lantern. He hated the idea of destroying someone else's property, but if he could set the wagon on fire, the blaze might distract the outlaws just long enough for him to reach the warehouse.

The only problem with the plan was that he couldn't find a lantern. And the snow-covered canvas wouldn't burn very well by itself . . .

Then his fingers made out the shape of a glass jug. Pulling it from the wagon, Fargo found that it had a cork in its neck. He worked the cork free, took a sniff of the contents, and grinned. He had thought the jug contained whiskey, but what was inside it was even better.

Kerosene.

Fargo worked quickly. He used the knife he had taken from Milo to cut a long strip from the canvas cover of the wagon. He rolled up the stiff fabric and stuck it in the neck of the jug, soaking it in the kerosene, then reversed the makeshift fuse and reinserted it, leaving about six inches hanging out. He found a lucifer and was about to light the fuse when he caught sight of movement from the corner of his eye. Three men had just come around the next wagon in line, and they spotted him crouching there. "It's Fargo!" one man yelled. "Get him!"

They opened fire as Fargo threw himself under the wagon and rolled toward the other side. Bullets kicked up snow and dirt where he had been a second earlier. He had the jug in one hand and the lucifer in the other, but he'd been forced to leave the rifle behind. He would have to make do with the weapon he still had.

He snapped the lucifer to life with his thumbnail, jammed the flame against the kerosene-soaked canvas, and tossed the jug into the path of the outlaws. All he could do was hope that the snow wouldn't put out the fuse before it reached the volatile liquid in the jug.

It didn't. The outlaws had time to recognize that something awful was underfoot, and one of them let out a wild yell just as the fire reached the kerosene and touched it off. The jug exploded like a bomb. The blast wasn't particularly loud, but it sprayed razor-sharp shards of glass. Even worse, brilliant fingers of flame reached out to engulf the three men who had thought they had Fargo cornered. They screamed in agony as the burning kerosene set them ablaze.

Nobody was going to be paying much attention to the warehouse now, Fargo thought as he came to his feet and dashed toward the log building. Behind him, the trio of outlaws staggered around like human torches, screeching out their death agonies.

Fargo was twenty feet from the door of the warehouse when he stopped short. Corrigan had appeared in the doorway, one arm wrapped around Maureen's neck, the other hand clutching a gun shoved against her head. Blood dripped from Corrigan's gun arm, but his grip on the pistol was steady enough. Fargo knew then that he had only grazed Corrigan with his earlier shot.

"Nice try, Fargo!" Corrigan called, raising his voice to be heard over the shrieks of the burning men. "I still got something you want, though."

One by one, the outlaws lost consciousness and fell silent, pitching forward. The flames that had consumed them sizzled out as they landed in the snow. Fargo heard the grisly sounds and knew that he didn't have to worry about them anymore. Corrigan couldn't have more than one or two men left. Fargo had whittled down the odds until they were almost even, but it hadn't been enough. Corrigan still held a hole card that Fargo couldn't beat.

Maureen.

"You bastard," Corrigan rasped. "You shot me!"

"Seemed like the thing to do at the time," Fargo said. After everything that had happened, to be so close to winning and then be denied was maddening, but he knew he had to keep a cool head. He was still alive, and Milo might be, too, so they had a chance.

"I ought to blow this bitch's brains out right in front of you. It'd serve you right for what you've done to me and my boys."

"You brought it on yourself, Corrigan," Fargo said. "But it's over now. You're all alone. The only one left. Your gang can't help you now."

Corrigan shook his head. "That ain't right. I still got some of my boys." He raised his voice again. "Quint! Asa! McPherson! Sterling! Where the hell are you?"

"Hell's right," a new voice said. Fargo didn't dare take his eyes off Corrigan, but he knew who had spoken. Milo came limping out from behind the wagons. "That's where they are. They're all dead but you, Corrigan."

"No," Corrigan said, his voice trembling a little now. "It ain't possible. You're nothin' but a bunch o' helpless greenhorns . . ."

Milo stood shoulder to shoulder with Fargo now. "That's what you thought," Fargo said to Corrigan. "But you figured wrong."

Corrigan's face twisted with madness and rage. He jerked the gun away from Maureen's head and pointed it toward Fargo and Milo. They couldn't shoot as long as the outlaw was using her as a shield, but Maureen took care of that, driving an elbow back into Corrigan's midsection and breaking his grip. She tore free from him and dove to the side as Corrigan fired. The bullet went between Fargo and Milo.

Fargo reached behind and palmed the Colt from the small of his back. At the same time, Milo brought the rifle he carried to his shoulder. Both men fired and kept firing, the shots blending together to form one long, continuous roll of gun thunder. Corrigan was picked up by the slugs smashing into him, his feet coming completely off the ground as the tremendous impact of the bullets threw him backward. He thudded onto his back, shot to pieces, dead as dead can be.

Maureen lay on the ground a few feet away, saying softly over and over, "My God, my God, my God . . ."

Fargo lowered his smoking pistol but kept it pointing in the general direction of Corrigan. Even when a foe had been hit numerous times, it was Fargo's habit not to assume a man was dead until he had checked for himself. He went forward slowly, Milo beside him, and trained the Colt on Corrigan. The light from the warehouse showed the outlaw leader's sightless, staring eyes and the bloody ruin that had been his chest. That chest was motionless in death.

"It's over," Milo said. "It's really over." He sounded like he couldn't believe it.

Fargo understood the feeling. So much had happened in such a short period of time; it was hard to comprehend that the danger was finally past.

He holstered the Colt and stepped over quickly to Maureen. Dropping to a knee, he reached out and touched her shoulder, saying her name. She jerked back with a gasp, then looked up at him as understanding and relief flooded her face. "Oh, Skye!" she exclaimed. She rose up and threw her arms around him, hugging him tightly.

Fargo returned the embrace. "It's all right, Maureen," he told her. "Corrigan's dead, and so are the rest of the outlaws. They can't hurt anybody anymore."

She sobbed against his chest for a moment, then sniffled and tried to compose herself. "I . . . I was so scared . . ."

"We all were. But that was fast thinking, getting out of the way like you did."

Milo came up behind them. "Maureen, are you all right?" he asked, an edge of worry in his voice.

She leaned back to look up over Fargo's shoulder at

her former brother-in-law, and managed to put a smile on her tear-streaked face. "I'm fine," she assured him. "I was afraid, when Corrigan came in there and grabbed me, but he didn't really hurt me."

"What about the others?" Fargo asked.

"They're all right. Still a little shocked by everything that's happened, of course." Maureen wiped away tears. "We all are. But it's over now."

Fargo nodded and got to his feet, helping her up as well. They turned toward the warehouse along with Milo, and as the three of them approached the door, Ed Dugan appeared there.

"Them was some fireworks," the old trapper said. "I never saw the like of them three owl hoots burnin' up."

It would be all right with him, Fargo thought, if he never saw anything like that again. Those men had chosen to ride the outlaw trail, but meeting such a fiery end was still an awful way to die.

Of course, he reflected, there weren't too many *good* ways to die. But in the end, it never mattered much how a man left this world. What was important was the way he had lived in it.

And on that score, Skye Fargo hoped he didn't have too much to worry about.

11

There was a lot to do before morning. Fargo saw to it that guns were passed out among all the emigrants while Maureen bandaged a fresh bullet gash in Milo's arm from his last shoot-out with one of Corrigan's men. After checking on the Ovaro and making sure the big stallion and the rest of the livestock were all right, Fargo led a detail of men that gathered up the bodies of all the outlaws and placed them in one of the cabins. The whole gang had been accounted for, Fargo noted, and all bodies recovered, except for those of Griffith and Myers, who had been torn to pieces by the Lost River Lurker.

That thought made Fargo wonder again what had happened to the creature, and he stayed alert despite the weariness that gripped him. There had been no sign of the Lurker since it fled over the stockade wall earlier, but that didn't mean it couldn't come back. However, Fargo's instincts no longer sensed the oppressive nearness of the creature, as they had earlier. He felt—he hoped—it was gone for good.

He wasn't the only one interested in the Lurker. After the corpses of the outlaws had been piled in the cabin, Ed Dugan came over to Fargo and asked, "Whatever happened to the big critter?"

"I don't know," Fargo replied honestly. "The last I saw of it, it was climbing over the wall."

"Was it hit durin' all that shootin'?"

Fargo nodded. "I'm pretty sure Corrigan tagged it

with that Sharps of yours. Some of the others hit it with pistol and rifle fire, too."

Dugan scowled. "But you say the varmint got up and walked away?"

"It did more than that. After Corrigan knocked it down with the Sharps, it got up and came after me. I reckon I'm lucky I've still got my head and the rest of me is in one piece."

"Yeah, I reckon," Dugan said slowly as he nodded. "It takes a whole hell of a lot to hurt the Lurker."

Fargo thought of something else. "Earlier tonight, when we were holed up in that cabin, you said something about going out the back way. I know now what you meant."

Dugan shifted his feet and looked a little uncomfortable. "You do?"

"Yeah. I found that hidden door in the chimney. How'd you know about that, Dugan?"

The old trapper bristled a little at being questioned. "Well, why wouldn't I? I done told you, I been around this part of the country for nigh on to thirty years. Spent many a winter in this here fort. I know ever'thing there is to know about it."

"Does it have any more secrets like that door?"

"Not that I know of."

"Who built it? Why's it there in the first place?"

"The fella who built it was one o' the first trappers up here in these parts," Dugan explained. "He said he always felt a mite uncomfortable in a place with only one way in and out, so when he put up the cabin and mortared the chimney together, he came up with a way to hide that door in it. The Injuns had a habit sometimes of usin' flamin' arrows to set fire to a place and run a fella out into the open so's they could finish him off. The gent who built the cabin had a powerful fear o' burnin' up, so he thought it'd be fittin' to have a bolt hole so's he could escape a fire by goin' through the fire. Or the fireplace, I reckon you could say." Dugan wiped the back of his hand across his mouth. "That's more'n I've talked in pert near a year. I could use a drink."

"This man you're talking about," Fargo persisted, curious now. "What happened to him?"

"Oh, he's dead now," Dugan said without hesitation. "Been dead for years." The lined old face became more solemn. "Reckon it's a good thing he weren't here tonight to see those owl hoots burn up the way they did. I don't think he could've stood it. The sight would've made him pure crazy."

"It was bad enough I won't forget it for a long time, either," Fargo said.

The sky was turning gray in the east with the approach of dawn. The long night—one of the longest in Fargo's life—was nearly over. And suddenly the exhaustion, the aches and pains that filled his body, were all too much to bear. He had to get some rest. He told Dugan he would see him later, then turned toward one of the empty cabins. His breath fogged in front of his face in the frigid air. The temperature was well below freezing. The ground under its thick layer of snow probably was frozen too hard already to allow the dead men to be buried. He would have to find a deep ravine somewhere nearby, Fargo thought, and drop the corpses in it before covering them with rocks. That really wouldn't be a proper burial, but it was the best Fargo could do under the circumstances.

Before he could reach the cabin, he saw Maureen moving to intercept him. Her arms were full of something, and as Fargo came closer, he recognized it as one of the buffalo robes. Maureen smiled at him as she said, "I thought you might be tired and want to sleep for a while, Skye, so I decided I'd bring you this. It's awfully cold."

Fargo nodded and returned her smile. "Yes, it is. I'm much obliged."

"Are you going in that cabin? I'll gather some wood and make a fire, too."

"That's not necessary," Fargo started to tell her, but she stopped him by shaking her head.

"If not for you, Corrigan would have killed all of us sooner or later. You need to let us take care of you for a while."

Fargo grinned. "I'd argue with you . . . but I'm too damned tired."

He took the buffalo robe, draped it around his shoulders, and went into the cabin. Like all the others in the fort, it was unfurnished, with only a fireplace and a dirt floor. Fargo stretched out and rolled up in the thick robe while Maureen bustled around, bringing in wood and lighting a fire in the fireplace. Fargo hadn't been aware of just how cold he really was until he began to warm up. Then he felt the sharp ache of the freezing temperatures that had crept into his bones. He sighed as sleep nibbled at the edges of his consciousness.

His last thought was that he had forgotten to ask the old trapper who Arthur Dugan was, or more than likely, had been. That wasn't important, though, Fargo told himself as he dozed off. It could wait until later.

Fargo's sleep was deep and dreamless, and he had no idea how long it lasted. All he knew was that he came awake instantly, as he always did when something disturbed his senses. His hand shot out of the warm folds of the buffalo robe and closed over the butt of his Colt, which he had reclaimed along with his Henry rifle and Arkansas toothpick from the gang's stash of weapons.

Fargo rolled over sharply, bringing up the revolver as he did so. His thumb drew back the hammer as he lined the barrel on the figure just inside the cabin door.

"Don't shoot, Skye!" Maureen exclaimed. "It's just me."

Fargo was holding his breath. He blew it out in a long sigh as he carefully let down the hammer of the Colt. He lowered the gun and slid it back in its holster.

"Sorry," he said. "Old habits are hard to break."

"I don't want you to break them," Maureen said as she came farther into the cabin and closed the door behind her. She was carrying a lit candle. "After all, they've helped keep you alive this long, haven't they?"

Fargo grinned. "Yeah, I reckon you could say that."

"I should have knocked. Actually, I did, but I suppose I should have knocked harder. You must have been sleeping so soundly that you didn't hear me."

Fargo stretched his arms above his head and rolled his shoulders, trying to work out the kinks in his muscles. "What time is it, anyway?" he asked.

"It's night again. The sun went down a little while ago."

Fargo grunted in surprise. He had slept the entire day away. It hadn't felt like it. "Did you get any rest?"

"Yes, I did. I feel a lot better now." She came closer to him. "I was wondering if you were hungry."

"As a matter of fact, my belly's so empty it thinks my throat's been cut."

"Oh. I see." Maureen set the candle on the mantel above the fireplace, where the blaze of earlier in the day had died down to embers that still gave off some heat. Her fingers went to the top button of her dress. "You don't need to work up an appetite, then," she said with a smile as she toyed with the button for a second and then unfastened it.

Fargo felt an immediate reaction at the sensuousness of her smile and the look of passion in her heavy-lidded eyes. "I didn't say that," he told her. "A fella's appetite can always use a little whetting."

Maureen undid the second button on her dress. "That's what I thought," she murmured as she sank to her knees on the robe beside him.

Fargo's fingers took the place of hers as he slowly unfastened several more buttons and spread her dress open. He slid his hands inside the garment and cupped her breasts through the long underwear she wore under the dress. He felt her nipples harden against the palms of his hands.

Maureen closed her eyes and whispered his name as he caressed her. Fargo leaned closer to her and brought his mouth to her slightly parted, inviting lips. The kiss was sweet and hot, and she opened eagerly to his probing tongue. Her hands rested on his chest and clutched at his buckskins as he tightened his grip on her breasts.

"We have too many clothes on," she said when they finally broke the kiss.

"That's just what I was thinking," Fargo agreed with a smile.

They undressed each other, taking turns baring each other's body. The air in the cabin was chilly but not uncomfortably cold. When Maureen's breasts were revealed, the nipples stood out in hard, straining urgency. She looked down at them and laughed. "I think they'd be like that no matter what the temperature was," she said. "You have that effect on me, Skye."

"You have a pretty strong effect on me, too," he told her as he lifted his hips so that she could pull his trousers down over them. His erection tented the front of his underwear.

Maureen laughed happily again and said, "So I see." She stroked his shaft through the underwear and then pulled them down as well. Fargo's organ jutted proudly from his groin.

Maureen put both hands around the long, thick pole and lowered her head over it. Her tongue darted out and licked warmly around the crown, lapping up the pearl of moisture that beaded on the end. Then she opened her mouth even wider and let it engulf him. Several inches of his shaft disappeared into the hot, wet cavern. She tightened her lips, swirled her tongue around the head several times, and then began to suck gently.

Fargo closed his eyes and luxuriated in the pleasure Maureen was giving him. After everything that had happened, all the trouble and danger he had been through over the past few days, it felt absolutely wonderful just to lie back and enjoy what she was doing to him. After a while, though, it seemed that he was getting the better end of the deal, and that wasn't fair. He took hold of Maureen's hips and growled in a voice husky with need, "Come here."

She positioned herself over him as he stripped away the last of her clothes. Her lips still moved over his groin as she straddled his head with her knees. In the candle-light, he had a perfect view of her femininity, the folds pink and glistening with her dew, surrounded by soft, thick brown hair. Fargo used his thumbs to spread the folds and then lifted his head to lick teasingly along her opening. She couldn't speak because her mouth was full of his manhood, but she made a moaning sound of satisfaction deep in her throat.

Then Fargo speared his tongue into her. Her hips bucked in response, and her hands tightened on his shaft. She began sucking harder as she thrust her femaleness against his face. Fargo delved as deeply within her as he could, while at the same time cupping and squeezing the fleshy globes of her rear end.

After several minutes of this, Maureen lifted her head with a gasping cry. "Oh, my God, Skye, I can't stand it! I need you in me!"

Fargo was glad to oblige. He steadied her as she swung around and positioned herself above him, her hips poised to descend on his waiting manhood. Fargo let her set the pace. Maureen bit her lip and visibly struggled for control as she lowered herself slowly onto his heated, throbbing shaft, inch by inch. When she finally had all of it sheathed within her, her hips began a languorous pumping. Smiling, she leaned forward over Fargo's torso so that her breasts dangled within reach of his mouth. He caught one nipple between his lips and teased it with his tongue, then the other. Maureen stroked his head tenderly.

Fargo reached around her, rested his hands on her rump as it rose and fell. His member slid in and out of her, and as the excitement mounted for both of them, their movements grew faster and faster. Fargo thrust up to meet her, and their groins slapped together with each downward stroke of her hips. Their lovemaking was pure and instinctive, a simple giving and taking of pleasure and comfort that filled them both with the need to draw closer and closer. Fargo felt his climax building and didn't try to hold back, knowing that Maureen was ready for it. His back arched and he thrust into her a final time, plumbing her depths to the utmost of his ability as he began to spasm. She cried out as her own fulfillment shook her, and Fargo emptied himself inside her, filling her to overflowing.

Only when he had given her all he had to give did he let himself relax. Maureen sagged forward at the same time, sprawling on his broad, muscular chest. The top of her head came just below his chin. He reached up and stroked her smooth, dark hair with one hand while the other rested just below the small of her back, at the top of her cleft.

After a few moments of contented silence, Maureen said, "It feels so good just lying here with you, Skye." She snuggled closer to him, flattening her breasts against his chest. "The way you breathe is so soothing, I could go right to sleep."

Fargo chuckled.

Maureen lifted her head. "What's so funny?"

"I've been called a lot of things in my life," Fargo said, "but I don't recollect the last time anybody told me I was *soothing*."

She balled one small hand into a fist and thumped him playfully on the breastbone. "Well, doggone it, you are!"

"What I am is hungry."

"Oh, your appetite is whetted properly now, is it?"

"I reckon," Fargo said.

Maureen laughed. "I'm pretty wet, too, when you get right down to it. And we certainly did, didn't we?"

"Yes, ma'am," Fargo agreed. His belly let out a loud rumble.

Maureen looked alarmed. "You really *are* starving, aren't you?"

"I could eat," Fargo admitted.

Still straddling his hips, she pushed herself into a sitting position. The move made her breasts bounce enticingly, and the sight caused his shaft to give a little jump and swell slightly. It was still inside her, so she couldn't help but feel the reaction.

"Not now," she said firmly. "As much as I'd like to do that again, we need to get some food in you. Come on, Skye, let's get dressed."

With mixed emotions and not a little reluctance, he nodded his agreement.

Over the next few minutes, Fargo discovered that it was almost as enjoyable watching Maureen put on her clothes as it was watching her take them off. When they were both dressed, they left the cabin and walked toward the warehouse. Maureen carried the candle to light their way.

"Everyone has stayed in the warehouse except Mr. Dugan," she said. "And you, of course. After everything that happened, I don't think anyone wanted to be alone. We all liked having the whole group around."

"I can understand that," Fargo said. "What about Corrigan and his bunch?"

"They're still, ah, where you left them. That's all right, isn't it?"

Fargo nodded. "It probably didn't get much above freezing today, if any. They'll keep for a day or two, and by that time, I'll have found a ravine where we can put them."

"We can't bury them?"

"Starting a rock slide to cover them up will be the best anybody can do before next spring, and by then I hope we're all long gone from here."

"You don't think we'll have to stay here all winter?"

"That's still possible," Fargo admitted. He sniffed the air. "I've got a hunch the wind's going to turn around to the south, though, and that'll give us one last spell of warm weather before winter sets in good and proper. If it does, the snow in the pass will melt enough for us to get through, and we'll head for Fort Hall."

After a moment, Maureen said, "I don't really know what to hope for. So many terrible things have happened here, and yet . . ."

Fargo knew she was thinking about the times they had made love here. He took her free hand and squeezed it. "I know what you mean." It was like everything else in

137

life, triumph and tragedy intermixed, and all a fella could do was hope that in the end, the good outweighed the bad.

He recalled her saying something about Dugan not being at the warehouse. He asked, "Where's the old-timer gotten off to?"

"You mean Mr. Dugan? I'm not sure. He said something about going out and looking for some fresh meat."

Fargo frowned. "And he went alone?"

"Yes." Maureen's tone echoed his concern as she went on, "I know what you're thinking, Skye. You're worried about that creature . . . that Lost River Lurker, as Mr. Dugan calls it."

"We don't know if it's still around or not. I'm pretty sure it was wounded, but that might just make it worse, if that's possible."

"I know, but Mr. Dugan wouldn't be talked out of it. He said he knew the country around here better than anyone else, even the Lurker. And he said that even if they ran into each other, the Lurker wouldn't hurt him."

"Huh," Fargo said. "I'd like to know why he thinks that. It didn't seem to me that the thing was too choosy about who it tore up."

"It didn't hurt me," Maureen reminded him. "It just looked at me and then . . . well, went away. Without harming me or even touching me."

"True enough," Fargo admitted. "I know how it got in and out of that cabin, too." He explained to her about the hidden door in the chimney. "I guess anybody who's been around these mountains long enough knows that secret, even a thing like the Lurker."

"What do you think it really is?"

Fargo had to shake his head. "I honestly don't know. Nothing like I ever saw before, that's for sure."

When they reached the warehouse, everyone gave Fargo a warm welcome. The young blond girl Maggie came up to him and put her arms around him in a heart-felt hug. "Thank you," she said.

"If I remember right," Fargo told her, "it was that

critter screeching outside that made Corrigan leave you alone, Miss Maggie."

"But you're the one who killed that evil man," she insisted. "All of us owe you more than we can ever repay, Mr. Fargo."

Maggie's mother said, "My daughter is right, Mr. Fargo," and the girl's father clasped Fargo's hand and pumped it up and down for what seemed like several minutes. Being the object of such adulation made Fargo more than a little uncomfortable. He was glad when they went on about their business.

The air was filled with delicious aromas coming from a big iron cook pot suspended over the fire in the center of the room. One of the women brought Fargo a bowl of stew and a cup of strong black coffee. Someone had carried in a bench from one of the wagons. Fargo was ushered over to it and seated on it like a king being forced to take the throne by his adoring subjects.

Maureen sat down beside him as he dug into the stew. It tasted as good as it smelled. Fargo had to force himself not to wolf it down. He ate slowly, sipped the coffee, and felt the strength from both seeping back into his body. A few more meals like this and he would start to feel downright human again.

When he finished the stew, Maureen started to get to her feet, saying quickly, "Let me get you some more."

Fargo halted her with a hand on her arm. "You've got to stop carrying on so over me, Maureen," he told her in a quiet voice. "And so does everybody else. A lot of bad things happened, but we pulled through them together. That's the way it's supposed to be." That reminded him of something, and he looked around for a second before he went on, "Where's Milo?"

Maureen looked for him as well and frowned when she didn't see him. "I don't know. He was here when we came in. I saw him."

Fargo hadn't noticed him, but he was willing to take Maureen's word that Milo had been in the warehouse. He wasn't now, however.

"Must have gone outside to take a look around. Are there any guards keeping an eye on things?"

"Well, not really. Milo was worried that the Lurker might come back, and he thought everyone would be safer if they stayed in here together. I know he was upset that I went to fetch you to supper by myself."

Fetching him for supper wasn't the only reason Maureen had come to the cabin where he was sleeping, Fargo thought. And Milo had been right that she shouldn't have gone over there alone. Having a few guards along for company would have put a definite crimp in Maureen's plans, though.

Fargo could understand as well the reluctance of the emigrants to spread out among the cabins in the fort. There was safety in numbers, they reasoned—although so far during their journey, that old adage hadn't held true all the time. They had been together when Corrigan's gang held them up and then later made them prisoners, and it hadn't helped much. For the time being, it was all right for them to stay here in the warehouse as a group. If they had to spend the winter, though, after a while the quarters would get awfully cramped. Then they would have to spread out again, whether they liked it or not.

Fargo sat there and talked to people as they drifted past, but he soon became restless. He stood up and said, "I think I'll go take a look around for Milo."

"I'll come with you," Maureen said without a second's hesitation.

"I don't know if that's a good idea . . ."

"Just try to talk me out of it," she told him with a teasing smile.

Fargo smiled back at her. "I wouldn't waste the time and trouble," he said.

He picked up a rifle and went to the door with Maureen beside him. They stepped out into the cold, clear night. Overhead, stars glittered brilliantly in the sable sky. "It'll be cold again tonight," Fargo said. "Bitter cold. But tomorrow, the wind turns around and it starts to warm up."

"Can you really predict the weather?"

"After you've lived out here on the frontier long enough, you get a feeling for things. I could be wrong, but I think the snow will melt enough for the wagons to get through the pass."

"I hope so. As nice as some of our time here has been, I'd rather spend the winter in what passes for civilization."

Fargo chuckled. "Fort Hall's not all that civilized. I reckon it beats the middle of nowhere, though."

He hadn't seen any sign of Milo Haydon so far, but the gate in the stockade wall swung open suddenly and a lean figure slipped through the gap. The starlight was bright enough for Fargo to recognize the thick coat and the fur cap. "Dugan," Fargo called. "Where have you been?"

Dugan stepped toward them, but before the old trapper could answer Fargo's question, flame lanced out from behind one of the wagons. Echoes of the shot resounded in the thin air. Dugan staggered and fell.

Fargo let his instincts take over. He pushed Maureen aside, getting her out of the line of fire as his hand flashed toward the butt of the gun on his hip. As fast as he was, though, he couldn't outdraw an already drawn gun. Another blast shattered the night air, and what felt like a giant fist slammed into Fargo's belly. As if from a great distance, he heard Maureen screaming as he doubled over and fell to his knees. He tried to lift his gun, but it slipped from his fingers.

Fargo heard a guttural curse, then a slap as a hand cracked sharply into flesh. "Shut up!" a familiar voice ordered. "You're comin' with me."

"Milo, no!" Maureen cried out, and then he hit her again, silencing her.

Fargo managed to lift his head as he hung on grimly to consciousness. He saw the dark figure looming over him, heard the gloating voice as Milo Haydon said, "Mr. Damned High and Mighty Trailsman. You don't look like so much now, do you, Fargo? I ought to put a bullet through your head for what you've done. Try to steal Maureen away from me, will you? She's *my* woman, mine! And she always will be!"

Fargo tried to find the strength to come up off the ground and lunge at Milo. In another second or two, he might have been able to do it. But then Milo swung the rifle in his hand and cracked the barrel across the side of Fargo's head, sending him tumbling into the snow.

"You're gut-shot," Milo said brutally. "I'm goin' to leave you here to die long and slow and painfullike, Fargo. Just like you tried to do to me."

Faintly, very faintly, Fargo heard the sounds of Maureen struggling as Milo dragged her away. He wanted to get up and go after them, but by now darkness was flooding in all around his consciousness, blotting out the stars overhead one by one. The last of them went out, and so did Fargo.

12

The pain in his belly was the first sign Fargo had that he was still alive. It grew and swelled, filling him, driving out the darkness that had claimed him. He became aware of other things: the cold that gripped him, and the babble of voices.

Then a hand lightly slapped his cheek, and he opened his eyes to look up into the lean, grim face of Ed Dugan.

"I knew you was alive," the old trapper said. "You're like me, Fargo—hard to kill."

The wet cold underneath Fargo told him that he was lying in the snow. He groaned and tried to sit up. The pain in his midsection was too much for him to overcome, however. He slumped back down.

"Take it easy for a minute," Dugan said. "I reckon you must feel like you been kicked in the gut by a mule. Here, maybe this'll help."

He put a flask to Fargo's lips. Fargo swallowed some of the raw whiskey that spilled into his mouth. The liquor burned all the way down his gullet and then exploded in his stomach, but the fiery stuff gave him strength and numbed some of the pain. He tried to pull himself upright again, and this time he made it.

"Maureen?" he rasped.

"Gone," Dugan said. "Nobody knows what happened to her."

"I do. Milo took her. That bastard."

"You mean Haydon?" Dugan asked in surprise. "He's the one who shot me?"

"And me," Fargo said. He put a hand to his belly, expecting to find his buckskins sodden with blood. Instead, they were dry. That discovery made Fargo frown in confusion.

"You ain't shot," Dugan told him. "I reckon the son of a bitch tried, but all he hit was this." Dugan held up something in his hand, and in the starlight, Fargo recognized it as the pepperbox pistol he had taken from the hiding place in the cabin. He had meant to give it back to Dugan earlier, but it had still been tucked behind Fargo's belt when Milo attacked him. The gun's breech was smashed.

Dugan went on, "You're a lucky man, Fargo. This ol' pepperbox saved your life."

"What about you? I saw Milo shoot you."

"The fella ain't as good of a shot as he thinks he is. His bullet tore a chunk o' meat outta my side, and I reckon I passed out for a little while on account o' losin' so much blood, but I'm all right. Takes more'n a little scratch like that to lay low a leathery old cuss like me."

Fargo looked around. Quite a few of the emigrants were standing in a circle around him and Dugan. They had been asking questions earlier, but now they were quiet, no doubt shocked by Fargo's assertion that Milo was to blame for this latest outrage.

He climbed to his feet. "They'll have left plenty of tracks in the snow. We can follow them."

Dugan nodded. "That's just what I was thinkin'."

One of the men stepped forward and said, "Mr. Fargo, you and Mr. Dugan are both hurt. You can't find Milo and Maureen in your condition."

"I can't stand around and wait for him to bring her back," Fargo said. "That's not going to happen. Something's happened to Milo. He's lost his ability to think straight."

And yet, even as Fargo spoke, he wondered if Milo had been that way all along. At times, Milo had seemed to be a staunch ally, as when they were battling Corrigan and his gang. But before that, he had never bothered to conceal his dislike for Fargo, and Fargo remembered as well the casual way Milo·had slashed the throats of the two unconscious outlaws. A man could have many faces. Maybe Milo had succeeded in masking the insane one—until tonight.

Moving gingerly because of the pain in his belly, Fargo began saddling the Ovaro while Dugan did likewise with his old mule. The trapper had gone out on foot to hunt and had brought back the carcass of a young deer, which some of the emigrants hauled into the fort to skin and dress out. Fargo told Maggie's father to take charge of the group while he and Dugan were gone.

"If we don't make it, it'll be up to you to see that the wagons get back to Fort Hall," Fargo told the man. "Come the spring, you can hire another guide there to take you the rest of the way to Oregon."

The man swallowed nervously. "How will we know if we can get through the pass?"

"You'll have to check on it once the weather warms up—if it does." Fargo squeezed the man's shoulder reassuringly. "Maybe it won't come to that. I figure Dugan and I will be back with Maureen by sometime tomorrow."

Dugan snorted. "Damn right. Haydon don't know these mountains, and I do. He won't get away."

Fargo hoped that was the case. He hated to think of Maureen in the hands of that madman.

They rode out a short time later. The pain in Fargo's belly had subsided to a dull ache. He figured that he would have one hell of a bruise from the impact of the pepperbox being driven into his body by Milo's bullet. He could live with a bruise, though, especially considering how close he had come to death.

Since it wasn't snowing anymore and the winds were light, the tracks left by the horses carrying Milo and Maureen were still visible, even by starlight. The trail led straight up the Lost River Valley toward the mountains that closed off the upper end. Fargo wondered where Milo thought he was going, then decided there was a good chance Milo wasn't thinking at all. He was just running away and dragging Maureen along with him.

Fargo hoped he and Dugan could catch up to them before Milo harmed her. Milo claimed to love her, but in his addled state, there was no way of knowing what he was capable of.

The tracks showed that Milo was pushing the horses hard, even though he probably believed that Fargo and Dugan were both dead. Still, he didn't have much of a lead. Fargo thought it was possible he and Dugan would catch up before sunrise. That would be best, if they could do it, so that Milo wouldn't see them coming. They would stand a better chance of rescuing Maureen without any harm coming to her if they could take Milo by surprise.

It was far into the night when Fargo spotted something strange up ahead. The trail left by Milo and Maureen wavered a bit but generally ran straight. More tracks came in from the west, following a curving path that merged with the other trail. Fargo reined in and frowned at the new tracks. "What the hell?" he muttered.

Dugan pulled his horse to a stop beside Fargo and sighed. "I know that sign," the old trapper said. "It's the Lurker."

Fargo had been worried about that when he saw the gigantic size of the tracks. He swung down from the saddle, fished a lucifer from his coat pocket, and struck it, cupping the match flame in his other hand as he knelt. "Look there," he said, nodding toward a scattering of dark spots around the tracks. "The thing's bleeding."

"I was afraid of that. He was hit too many times, hit too hard."

Fargo heard something in Dugan's voice that made him turn his head and look up at the man. "You sound like you're sorry for it."

"Him," Dugan corrected. "Not it. Him. The Lurker is a man. *Was* a man, anyway."

Fargo straightened from his crouch. "I've had a hunch all along that you knew more about the Lurker than you were letting on. Don't you reckon it's about time you told me the truth?" He pointed at the tracks. "After all, it's following Maureen and Milo, too, just like we are."

"He won't hurt the girl," Dugan said. "He ain't that sort."

"You know that for a fact?"

"I know a lot of things," Dugan snapped. "And you're right, it's time I spilled 'em. But get back on your horse. We can talk while we ride."

That sounded like a good idea to Fargo. He mounted up, and he and Dugan rode north again, following the trail that was made more visible by the addition of the Lurker's footprints.

"Remember that trapper I told you about, the one who built the cabin with the secret door in the chimney?" Dugan said. "That fella is the one they call the Lost River Lurker."

"I've run into him a couple of times," Fargo reminded him. "He didn't act much like any man I've ever seen."

"You wouldn't act like a man, either, if you'd been livin' in these mountains like an animal for more'n twenty years!" Dugan stopped and drew a deep breath. "I don't mean to get testy," he went on. "But you got to understand . . . him and me, we was close once. That's how I know he'd never hurt me. There ain't much human thought left in him, but there's enough so he still knows me."

"What happened to him?"

"Just about the worst thing that ever could have," Dugan said. "Worse than dyin', that's for sure. Remember I told you how he felt about fire? Well, one day he was out checkin' on his traps when the Shoshone jumped him. Those red devils hauled him back to their village, and they decided to have some sport with him. They . . . they burned him." Dugan's voice faltered, and he had to force himself to go on. "Burned him all over his body. Not enough to kill him, mind you, just enough to make him go out of his mind from the pain. Then they . . . burned his face off. Tied him down and piled hot coals on his face until there wasn't nothin' left of it. Then they

147

turned him loose that way. Bastards. Instead o' puttin' a bullet through his brain, like they should have, they let him live—if you can call it that."

Dugan fell silent. Fargo was so struck by the horror of the story that for a moment he couldn't bring himself to speak. Finally, he said, "How did he wind up being the Lurker?"

"I found him, after what the Injuns done to him," Dugan replied hollowly. "Took care of him the best I could. Reckon I should've put him out o' his misery, but I couldn't bring myself to do it. So I helped him live, even though his mind was gone. He was always a big, healthy fella. Mighty big and strong. You saw that for yourself. His body healed, and what little was left of his face scarred over, but there was no way to fix what was inside his head. When he was strong enough, he ran away from me. I thought about goin' after him . . . hell, I thought about huntin' him down and killin' him like the animal he'd become . . . but I couldn't do it. I figured the mountains would take care of it. I never thought he'd live this long."

"So you let him wander around this valley for years, terrorizing people and killing them?" Fargo couldn't keep the anger out of his voice.

"You don't understand, Fargo. I know I done wrong. But sometimes it seems that wrong is the only thing you can do. That there ain't no answer that won't send you to hell, one way or t'other."

Fargo was silent. Obviously, the years of knowing the truth about the Lurker had been a torment to Dugan. Fargo knew it was impossible to crawl into another man's skin and feel things the way he did. Maybe it was best not to judge.

But of one thing, Fargo was certain. They had to catch up to Milo and Maureen before the Lurker did. Dugan might be sure that the creature—it was impossible for Fargo to think of it in any other way—wouldn't harm Maureen, but Fargo didn't share that confidence.

They pushed on. Fargo saw more of the dark splatters of blood on the snow. It was possible the Lurker wouldn't even catch up to Milo and Maureen before its wounds claimed it. In a way, Fargo hoped that would be the case. He didn't like the idea of Dugan being forced to choose between the Lurker and the rest of them. If that happened, Fargo wasn't absolutely sure which way Dugan would decide . . .

The stars took on an added brilliance as the sky around them darkened even more. Fargo thought of the old saying about how it was always darkest before the dawn. There was some truth to that. A few minutes later, the horizon to the east began to take on a gray tinge. In less than an hour, the sun would poke its shining face above the peaks of the Lost River Range, and a new day would begin.

Suddenly, Fargo's keen eyes picked out some dark shapes, far ahead. He leaned forward in the saddle. "There they are!"

"I see 'em," Dugan said. "Looks like they're runnin' from the Lurker."

It was true. Two of the shapes were ahead of the other, moving fast as they swung away from the river and toward the mountains. That was the wrong move, Fargo thought. If Milo had stayed on relatively level ground, there was a good chance the mounts he and Maureen rode could outrun the creature that pursued them. Once those horses reached the slopes, though, they would have to slow down, and the Lurker could cut the gap between them. Already, as Fargo and Dugan spurred their animals ahead, they could see that the creature was moving rapidly across the snow in great, ungainly bounds. Even having heard the story from Dugan, Fargo was hard put to find anything human in the way the thing moved.

The Ovaro galloped ahead, snow flying from its hooves. Dugan tried to keep up on his mule, but he fell steadily behind Fargo. Milo and Maureen were in the foothills now, slowing down in their flight as Fargo had known they would have to. They disappeared over the crest of a rise, and a few moments later, the Lurker followed them. Fargo was still at least a mile back. He wasn't sure he could reach them before the Lurker caught up. He urged the Ovaro on, getting all the speed he could from the magnificent stallion under these adverse conditions. The snow slowed everything down.

Fargo heard gunshots popping. The sounds were distinct in the clear, cold mountain air. His wind-whipped face grew bleak, but he pressed on.

A short time later, he topped the rise where he had last seen Milo, Maureen, and the Lurker. About half a mile ahead, a cliff jutted up, forming a shoulder at the base of a mountain in the Sawtooth Range. The light was still too bad for Fargo to make out many details, but he thought he saw figures climbing on foot along a path that rose on one side of the cliff. He kept the Ovaro moving, heading for the base of the cliff with all the speed the stallion could muster.

By the time he reached it, the sky was still mostly gray but streaked with pink and orange, and Fargo could see the climbing figures. Maureen was the highest, being forced on by Milo. The Lurker was some fifty yards below them, steadily closing in. Milo and Maureen had left their horses at the foot of the cliff when it blocked their path. With the monstrous creature pursuing them, it must have seemed to Milo that trying to go up the cliff was the only avenue of escape open to them. Fargo knew it was futile, though. Even if they made it to the top before the Lurker caught them, the creature could swoop down on them without difficulty once it reached the shoulder as well.

There was nothing he could do to help Maureen down here, Fargo thought. He pulled the Henry from his saddle and started climbing after them.

The path was steep enough in places that Fargo had to put his free hand down to keep his balance as he climbed. In other places he could almost walk upright. He hurried as much as he could while still being careful. If he slipped and fell and tumbled to the bottom, he could break an arm or a leg or both, and then he wouldn't be any good to anybody. He was within rifle range of the Lurker already and thought about trying to bring down the creature, but remembering that it had once been human, he couldn't bring himself to fire. He wasn't sure what he would do when he caught up. He couldn't reason with the Lurker; Dugan's explanation had made it clear that rational thought was beyond the former trapper now. The Lurker acted purely on instinct, like an animal. And it was dying already, if the amount of blood it had lost was any indication.

Nor could Fargo forget the threat that Milo had become. Milo might be even more dangerous than the Lurker, because he still had his human cunning, just none of the scruples that should have gone with it.

Fargo heard a faint cry and knew it came from Maureen. That spurred him to climb even faster. He was taking chances now, risks that might cost him his life if he slipped, but he couldn't afford to be careful anymore. Time had run out—for him, for Milo and Maureen, for the Lurker. Fate had brought all of them to this rocky cliff that had been swept clean of snow by the wind.

Fargo looked up and couldn't see any of the others. They had reached the top of the cliff. Maureen screamed again, and again a gun roared. Fargo drove for the top, the ache in his belly forgotten. He scrambled up the last few yards of the path and reached the flat, ledge-like shoulder of ground at the top of the cliff.

Milo and Maureen were running from the Lurker, but as Fargo watched, it closed in on them. Milo threw a terrified look over his shoulder and suddenly grabbed Maureen's arm and flung her behind him. She cried out as she lost her balance and fell right in the path of the charging monster. Fargo snapped the Henry to his shoulder, ready to pump as many bullets as he could into the Lurker if it went for her.

Instead, the creature leaped over her and kept on after Milo. Maureen stayed where she was, face pressed to the ground, arms crossed over her head, her back shaking with sobs.

Milo reached the end of the ledge. The slope rose

sheer, with no path, no way to climb, nowhere to run. Milo carried a rifle, and he brought the weapon up as the Lurker rushed at him. Flame spurted from the barrel as Milo fired again and again, emptying the rifle as fast as he could work the lever and pull the trigger.

The Lurker shuddered and staggered with each slug that thudded into its body. But it kept on, coming closer and closer to Milo. Its path was unsteady now, though, and some of its steps sent it veering dangerously close to the edge of the cliff. Milo kept pulling the trigger even though the rifle was empty. Fargo was close enough to see that his face was contorted with terror.

The Lurker fell to one knee, then rose ponderously and struggled on. It wasn't running now, and its staggering pace told Fargo that the creature was having trouble putting one foot in front of the other. The sky lightened more with the approach of dawn. Fargo saw that the Lurker wore a thick buffalo coat much like the one Ed Dugan wore. The Shoshone hadn't scalped him while he was their captive; he had all his hair, and it grew thick and tangled from his mutilated head.

Fargo reached Maureen and dropped quickly to a knee beside her. He pulled her up into a sitting position. She screamed and started to fight him, but he set his rifle aside and gripped her arms tightly, shaking her. "Maureen!" he said. "It's me, Maureen! Stop it! It's Fargo!"

Understanding and recognition dawned in her eyes, which were swollen and red-rimmed from crying. She threw her arms around his neck and held on tight. "Skye! He said you were dead, that he had k-killed you!"

"I'm fine," Fargo told her. "Are you all right?"

She managed to nod. "Milo didn't hurt me. But he's crazy, Skye. He . . . he said he killed Daniel!"

Fargo had wondered about that. Obviously, Milo had wanted Maureen for a long time. Had he wanted her badly enough to push his own brother into a flood-swollen river and then lie about what had happened? Fargo didn't doubt it now.

He patted Maureen on the shoulder and said, "Stay here. Dugan's on his way." Then he picked up his rifle and got to his feet.

"Skye!"

Fargo didn't look back as he started toward Milo and the Lurker. Maureen would be all right, and things still had to be settled.

"Get away from me!" Milo screamed at the Lurker as it closed in on him. "Get away!"

The Lurker, mortally wounded, stumbled and almost fell. Righting itself, it took another step toward Milo, long arms outstretched, hands like claws ready to rend and tear. But again the creature staggered, and this time it came too close to the edge. It teetered on the brink for a second, then plunged over and vanished.

Fargo heard a faraway cry and recognized it as Ed Dugan screaming, "Art! Nooooo!"

Abruptly freed from the menace of the Lurker, Milo Haydon began to laugh. He saw Fargo coming toward him, but he still laughed. "Fargo!" Milo shouted. "Might as well turn around and leave. You can't beat me! Nobody can beat me! Daniel found that out. Stupid bastard thought he could take Maureen away from me. I reckon I showed him!"

Fargo stopped about fifteen feet away from him. "You killed your own brother?"

"He deserved it! Just like you did! Why aren't you dead? I shot you."

Fargo shook his head. "Your luck ran out, Milo."

"Luck?" Milo echoed bitterly. "What luck? The woman I love can't wait to run off and rut with you like an animal!"

"You murdered her husband," Fargo pointed out. "You can't expect her to forgive that."

"Well, what about the others?" Milo demanded. "Ungrateful sons o' bitches! I did as much to save them from Corrigan as you did, but do they give me any credit? No! They've got to fall all over the damned Trailsman and tell him how wonderful he is! I've had enough of it! I'm going to kill you all! All of you, you hear!" He brought the rifle to his shoulder and pressed the trigger. The hammer clicked emptily. Milo lowered the weapon and stared at it uncomprehendingly.

It would have been easy, Fargo knew at that moment, to lift his own Henry and put a bullet between Milo's eyes. But it wasn't for him to punish the man. The law would do that. Milo would hang once they got back to Fort Hall. Fargo took a step toward him, saying, "Come on, Milo. It's all over—"

A dull boom echoed from the face of the mountain looming above. Milo's head seemed to explode as a .50 caliber slug bored through it. His body dropped like a puppet with its strings cut.

Fargo turned to look and saw Ed Dugan standing at the top of the path, slowly lowering the Sharps Big Fifty. Smoke curled from the muzzle of the rifle's barrel. Dugan turned away and started back down the cliff.

Fargo let the old trapper go. He hadn't passed judgment on Milo Haydon; he wasn't going to do so on Dugan, either.

He left Milo there and got Maureen, helped her to her feet and then assisted her down from the cliff. "Stay here with the horses," Fargo told her, then he walked along the base of the cliff to where Ed Dugan sat on the ground with the head of the Lost River Lurker pillowed on a bony thigh. The creature's broken body was stretched out in the snow next to Dugan. To Fargo's amazement, the massive chest still rose and fell raggedly. Dugan was crying, tears dripping from leathery cheeks to land on the ruined face of the thing that had once been Arthur Dugan. Fargo had figured that out at last.

But he wasn't prepared for what he heard next, as the Lurker opened his eyes, looked up at Dugan, and contorted his travesty of a mouth to utter, "Ed . . . wina?"

"I'm here, Art. I'm here. I've always been here."

The Lurker's eyes closed and a great sigh left his body, taking with it whatever was left of the soul of the man.

Edwina Dugan cradled her husband's head in her lap.

Fargo stood there silently for a long moment, watching the sun come up. The wind freshened and was warm, and he knew that soon the snow would begin to melt.

*Colorado Territory, 1861—
Murder and deceit run rampant, and the
unwary pay the supreme price.*

Skye Fargo was having a grand old time. He had three
queens and two fours lying facedown on the table in
front of him. Behind him was a buxom dove named
Molly skillfully massaging his neck and shoulders. At his
elbow stood a half-empty bottle of rotgut. Life didn't
get any better. Taking a long swig, he announced, "I
raise another twenty." He added the last of his poke to
the considerable pot and sat back, as poker-faced as a
granite slab.

Two players folded. That left the one they called Garner. Clad in a fine bearskin coat, he was a tall drink of

water with a chest as big around as a water barrel. He had been friendly enough during the game, but there was something about him, about his eyes in particular, that hinted he was a troubled man. "I'd never forgive myself if I didn't see this through, hombre," he remarked, and met the raise. "Let's see what you've got."

Fargo savored the moment. His cards had been cold until about half an hour ago, when his luck changed. Now there was close to sixty dollars in the pot, the most there had been all evening, and in a few moments it would be his. He flipped his hand over. "Read 'em and bawl like a baby."

"Not bad. Not bad at all," Garner said. "Most times a hand like that will do a man proud. But it's not enough." He laid out his own, card by card. "Maybe you'll want to shed a few tears yourself."

Fargo stared. "Four kings beat me all hollow," he admitted, and sighed. There went the last of his money. And any chance he had of renting a hotel room. Tipping the bottle to his mouth, he pushed his chair back. "Count me out, boys. I'm plumb broke." At least he still had his winsome companion. Wrapping his left arm around her slender waist, he started to guide her toward the bar.

"Hold on a second. Did I just hear correctly? You're tapped out?" Molly's button of a nose scrunched up as if she had caught a whiff of dead fish.

"Does it make a difference? We can go to your place after you're done here." Winking, Fargo pecked her on the cheek.

"What about the fancy meal you promised?" Molly's green eyes roved from the dusty crown of his white hat, down over his buckskin shirt and pants, to the tips of his scuffed boots. "I swear! Men are all alike! They have one thing and one thing only on their small minds." Peeved, she ran a hand through her flaming red hair. "After eight hours of work I'll be famished. No meal, no frolic in the hay." She sashayed off.

Fargo let out with another sigh. It wasn't his night. He was beginning to regret ever stopping in Denver. Sure, there were more saloons and doves here than just about anywhere west of Kansas City. But it took money to enjoy them. He might as well head for the stable where he had left his Ovaro and sleep in the stall. Letting more coffin varnish sear his throat, he made for the batwing doors.

It was hard to believe, but not all that long ago Denver had consisted of a bunch of tents and ramshackle cabins. Now, thanks to the discovery of gold, it was a bustling city whose name had been changed several times along the way. First known as Montana City, it became St. Charles, then Denver City, and now plain Denver.

Easterners were still pouring in, arriving daily by wagon train or stage or on horseback, all eager to make their fortune. Most were doomed to bitter disappointment. Many would die, victims of the elements or hostiles or human greed. But that didn't stop them from coming.

Fargo breathed deep. Wood smoke laced the cool night air, as did other, less fragrant odors. Turning left, he strolled along a boardwalk fronting a block of stores and saloons, his spurs jingling lightly. Every few steps he treated himself to more whiskey.

Light poured from dozens of windows, bathing a stream of humanity that ebbed to and fro. Townsfolk, gamblers, prospectors, miners, mountain men, and more were all indulging in Denver's infamous nightlife. During the day the city was a model of decorum, with wives and children free to stroll about as they pleased. But after the sun went down Denver underwent a change. The churchgoing segment of the population retired to their homes, and the wild and woolly element emerged from their lairs. Among them were human wolves who prowled the darkened byways in search of easy prey. Which is why Fargo's lake-blue eyes narrowed when he heard scuffling sounds from the mouth of an alley up ahead, and why his right hand drifted to the smooth grips of his Colt.

Other pedestrians were passing the alley and hardly gave it a second look. An older man, though, paused. He recoiled in horror, then made as if to enter but abruptly changed his mind, shoved his hands into his pockets, and kept on walking. As he went by Fargo he averted his face as if ashamed of himself.

The sounds grew louder. Fargo heard the distinct thud of blows mixed with sadistic cackles. He reached the alley and stopped to take another sip.

Four men ringed a skinny figure on the ground. They were a big, burly bunch, who at first glance might be mistaken for miners. But their tied-down holsters marked them as men who made their living with their guns, not with picks and shovels. They were taking turns kicking their victim and laughing whenever he grunted in pain.

It was none of Fargo's business. He went to move on. But then the figure on the ground raised a pale face and cried out, "Please, mister! Enough! I'm sorry!"

"I bet you are, brat!" responded one of the four, his brawny fists clenched. "I'll teach you to try to steal my money!"

"But I wasn't!" the boy cried. "All I did was bump into you!"

Fargo scowled. He could tell the kid was lying. Footpads and pickpockets were as thick as fleas on an old coon dog, and widely despised. The boy had brought the beating on himself for being so stupid.

"Sure you did!" the brawny man growled. "That's why your fingers were in my back pocket!" The man delivered a kick that doubled the boy in half. "You lying sack of puke. Bull Mulligan wasn't born yesterday!" He kicked the boy again, low down.

One of the others chortled. "Pound him into the dirt, Bull! Break every damn bone in his body!"

"That's exactly what I'm fixing to do, Pierce." Mulligan raised his right boot to stomp on the stripling's face.

Fargo couldn't say what made him do what he did next. Entering the alley, he said quietly, "I reckon that's enough. The boy has learned his lesson."

Bull Mulligan glanced around. Disbelief twisted his swarthy features. "Who the hell asked you to butt in?"

Pierce glared. "If you know what's good for you, stranger, you'll mind your own damn business."

The boy looked at Fargo. He was in agony, his teeth clenched, trying hard not to cry out. He didn't plead for help. He just looked.

Mulligan brought his boot crashing down. At the last instant the boy jerked his head aside but the heel caught him a glancing blow on the cheek, enough to daze him and start blood trickling from his nose. Bull Mulligan raised his leg to do it again.

"I said that's enough," Fargo warned.

Pierce and the others turned. "What's this kid to you, mister? Are the two of you in cahoots?"

"I've never seen him before." Fargo took another sip. He was mildly annoyed at himself for putting his life at risk for a petty thief. The gunmen were taking his measure, and the alley might erupt in gunfire at any moment.

Bull Mulligan shouldered past his friends and halted with his hands on his hips, his right hand inches from a Cooper revolver. "You don't look like a Bible-thumper. And you're sure as hell not a meddling do-good townsman. So give me one good reason why I should stop or get the hell out."

"Pick any reason you like. But you're done beating him."

"Is that a fact?" Bull Mulligan grinned at his companions, then stabbed for the Cooper.

Fargo had his Colt out and up before the other man cleared leather. He slammed the barrel against Mulligan's temple. For most that would be enough to flatten them. Bull Mulligan, though, was aptly named. The blow rocked him on his heels, but that was all. Fargo struck him a second time, then a third, and sprang back, covering the others as Mulligan oozed to the dirt like tree sap. "Anyone else?"

Pierce had started to claw at his six-gun, a Manhattan Navy pistol, but now he froze, stupefied by the outcome, his fingers hooked above his Smith and Wesson.

Fargo commanded, "Raise your hands! All of you!"

They hesitated. A crafty expression came over Pierce, and he growled, "You might get one or two of us but not all three. If we go for our guns, you're as good as dead."

Fargo hoped to avoid gunplay. He would rather bluff them into backing down. But from the way they stood there with their bodies as rigid as boards, their elbows partially crooked to draw, he could see it wasn't working. Then a strange thing happened. Their gazes drifted past him and a look of unease replaced their fury.

"What's going on here?"

The voice was familiar. Pivoting so his back was to a building, Fargo warily regarded the newcomer.

It was Garner. He had shoved his bearskin coat aside to reveal a nickel-plated, ivory-handled Remington, and he stood in the alley mouth glowering at the hard cases who ringed the boy. "I'm waiting for an answer," he prompted when no one responded right away.

"These four were kicking the kid into the ground," Fargo said, nodding at the youth. The boy had risen onto an elbow and gingerly pressed a palm to a split cheek.

"Why?" Garner demanded, staring hard at Pierce.

"It was Bull's doing!" Pierce bleated. "The kid tried to pick his pocket, so we hauled the runt in here and were teaching him the error of his ways when this bastard stuck his nose in. He pistol-whipped poor Bull."

Garner stalked past Fargo and poked Mulligan with a boot. "I'm impressed. There aren't many hombres who could do this," he said thoughtfully, and then raised his head to glower at Pierce and the others. "I can't leave you idiots alone for more than five seconds, can I?"

"You know them?" Fargo asked, but he was ignored.

Suddenly Garner advanced and grabbed Pierce by the front of the shirt. Shaking the smaller man as a grizzly might shake a marmot, Garner grated, "What did I tell you before I went to the saloon? What were my exact words?"

"Not to get into a ruckus or do anything to draw attention." Pierce was scared and it showed.

"Don't draw any attention," Garner repeated. In an amazing display of physical strength, he lifted the other man clear off the ground so they were nose-to-nose. "Tell me. What part of that didn't you understand?"

"Why are you taking this out on me?" Pierce squawked. "Bull's to blame! And he was provoked, I tell you!"

"Is that a fact?" Garner shoved Pierce against the other two gunmen with such force, all three nearly spilled to the dirt. "If you jackasses can't follow orders, maybe you'll be replaced with others who can." He wheeled toward the street. "Pick up that gob of spit and drag him with us. I'll tend to his worthless hide later." Pausing, he glanced at Fargo. "As for you, buckskin, I'd have done the same thing if I found them first. You're off the hook this time."

Fargo stepped to the boardwalk and watched them file around a corner. He twirled the Colt into its holster and was about to move on when the boy called out.

"Hold on there, mister! I want to thank you for helping me."

The boy was on his knees, an arm across his gut, fumbling with a cap that had fallen off in the scuffle. Grimacing, he pushed to his feet and shuffled over. Blood trickled from several cuts aside from the gash on his cheek and he had a knot on his forehead the size of a hen's egg. Gamely, he offered a grimy hand. "I'm Billy Arnold. I'm extremely pleased to make your acquaintance."

"I can't say the same," Fargo bluntly responded without shaking. "You nearly got me shot." He took a few steps but the boy gripped his sleeve.

"I didn't catch your name."

"That's because I didn't give it." Fargo continued on but in a few strides acquired a shadow at his right elbow.

"Any chance you can spare a dollar?" Billy Arnold asked. "I'm sorry to pester you like this but I honest-to-God haven't eaten in pretty near two days." As if it were trained to act up on cue, his stomach rumbled.

The kid had more gall than a drunk on the prod, Fargo reflected. "You can starve to death for all I care. Maybe if you found a job instead of picking pockets for a living, you could afford to buy some food." The boy went to speak but Fargo held up a hand, silencing him, and left him standing there with his mouth hanging open.

The mention of food set Fargo's own stomach to growling and he tried to silence it with whiskey. It didn't work. To make matters worse, he felt a rare headache coming on. The sooner he turned in, the better.

The stable was on a side street. Not far from it a young couple were locked in a heated embrace and paid no attention as Fargo ambled by. He was almost to the stable doors when he heard the soft patter of someone rushing up behind him, and thinking he was being attacked, he spun and drew.

"My word! Is this the thanks I get for chasing you down?" Molly had a shawl across her shoulders and was toting a handbag. Enticing perfume wreathed her like a fragrant cloud. Sniffing in irritation, she smoothed her shawl. "I thought you had better manners than most of the lunkheads I put up with."

"How was I supposed to know who it was?" Fargo returned the Colt to its holster. "What are you doing here, anyhow? If that bartender claims I didn't pay for the bottle, he's loco."

"I came to apologize for being rude."

Things were finally going Fargo's way. Of all the doves

at the Ace's High, Molly had attracted him most. With her lustrous red hair, an hourglass body most women would kill for, and a sultry face as smooth and unblemished as expensive china, she was the kind of woman a man would give his eyeteeth to spend ten minutes with. "I thought you had your heart set on a fancy meal," Fargo said.

"I did. But that's no excuse for how I treated you." Molly fussed with her bangs. "You were nice to me. You bought me all the drinks I wanted. And you weren't pawing me every second like most men do. So how about we go to your place and make ourselves comfortable?"

"My horse might not care for the company."

"Your horse?" Molly blinked, glanced at the stable, and laughed. "Oh. I get it. You really are flat broke, aren't you?" Grinning, she hugged him close, her more than ample bosom cushioned against his chest. "Fair enough. What say we go to my place instead? It's not much. But the bed is comfy and I might be able to rustle us up a bowl of leftover stew."

Fargo's stomach rumbled again, loud enough to be heard in Missouri.

"I'll take that as a yes," Molly joked, entwining her arm with his. "Permit me to lead the way."

East of the saloon district frame homes had sprouted like tidy rows of corn, some framed by white picket fences and boasting flower beds or tiny gardens. Molly rented a pair of rooms on the second floor of a house owned by a store clerk who turned in punctually every evening at seven.

"We have to be mighty quiet," she whispered. "My landlord's not a prude but he won't take kindly to my having a male visitor at this hour." Rummaging in her bag for a key, she inserted it into the lock.

Fargo went to follow her in, but stopped. A feeling came over him, a feeling of being watched, a sensation he often experienced in the wild and which he had learned to ignore at his peril. From under his hat brim he peered intently into the surrounding darkness for some sign of whomever was out there. He saw no one. He entered the apartment just as Molly lit a lamp and a rosy glow washed over a comfortably furnished room.

Fargo was closing the door behind him when he heard her gasp and exclaim, "What the hell are you doing here?" Whirling, he spied a man seated in a rocking chair in a far corner. The intruder wore an expensive brown suit, an immaculate bowler, and polished shoes. A silver chain to a pocket watch dangled from his vest. He was a man of means and, from the cold stare he bestowed on Fargo, quite unhappy to find Molly wasn't alone.

No other series has this much historical action!

THE TRAILSMAN

To order call: 1-800-788-6262